Publish or Perish?

PUBLISH OR PERISH?

H. J. Forest

GLENDALE

First published in Ireland 1991
by Glendale Publishing Ltd
1 Summerhill Parade
Sandycove
Co. Dublin

British Library Cataloguing in Publication Data
Publish or perish.
I. Forrest, H. J.
823.914 [F]

ISBN 0–907606–83–0

Origination by Wendy A. Commins,
The Curragh, Co. Kildare
Printed in Ireland by Colour Books Ltd., Dublin

*To Don for his encouragement and to Jonathon
for so much help.*

1

'And a quarter of Barry's tea, please, Mrs Burke.'

She took a pencil stub and totted up the prices on a piece of paper. 'That'll be four pounds eighty-nine, please, Mr Mitchell.'

He knew it was an outrageous price for a few groceries, but he handed over a ten-pound note without protest.

'I have *The Kerryman* for you.' She rooted under the counter and found the newspaper. 'That'll be five thirty-four altogether.'

She counted out his change and put his purchases in little plastic bags. 'You'll be there on Sunday?'

'I will, please God. It should be a grand game. Jack O'Shea was in top form in Thurles last week. Jim Ronayne will be no match for him at all.' He rearranged the contents of his briefcase to make room for the packages. 'Will you be going yourself, Mrs B?'

She shook her head. 'Mikey's brother will be coming up from Ardrahan and they'll be wanting to go to the match. Somebody has to mind the shop.'

'I may have to mind the shop myself. I'm supposed to be off this weekend, but in my job you never know.'

'Well, God is good, Mr Mitchell.'

He smiled to himself as he left the shop. The Burkes

overcharged scandalously, but he could well afford the extra few pence and he enjoyed the chat. On first coming to Dublin, nearly twenty years ago now, he'd missed the convenience of the village shop that sold everything from rubber boots to aspirin and had resented having to visit several shops to buy the few necessities of his life. The advent of the supermarkets had changed that, but they were too impersonal and he felt foolish pushing a trolley. Just when the problems of shopping were threatening to drive him to matrimony, little shops like Burke's had become a feature of the locality. They were mostly owned by village shopkeepers driven from the west by competition from chain stores where the race that proudly fought the foreign invader for eight centuries now happily bought soap powder and disposable nappies from British and Canadian supermarkets.

It was getting dark as Mitchell strolled up Rathmines Road. A stretch in the evenings had been noticeable for the last few weeks, but tonight threatening rain clouds were bringing an early dusk. A sharp March wind was dodging between the buildings and blowing litter and dust in small waves around his ankles. He quickened his pace, regretting his rash decision to leave the car at home this morning.

It was unusual for him to be able to leave the office by six o'clock, and he'd almost forgotten how to enjoy a night off. He bought an *Evening Herald*, to find out what was on television, but the thought of wasting an evening watching cops and robbers on the box didn't appeal to him. If the rain held off he might go for a good long walk after supper. He wasn't getting enough exercise these days and was becoming very unfit. After that he could drop into Lynch's for a pint before closing time. There shouldn't be too many of the lads there on a Thursday night and there would be no after-hours session. They'd

8

put him under fierce pressure, of course, knowing that old Paddy Lynch wouldn't let them stay on for the few extra pints, unless Mitchell was there as a sort of hostage should the local gardai happen to look in.

* * *

'Sorry, Brian, I didn't know you were here.' Catherine Gildea stuck her head round the door of the office.

'Catherine!' Brian Barry sounded startled and looked up from the notes he was writing. 'What are you doing here at this hour?'

'I saw the light but I thought it had been left on by mistake.' She leaned against the door-jamb, obviously ready for a chat.

'Aren't you going to the centenary function.'

'I had intended going, but young Maeve had to stay late to complete an experiment, so I'll have to wait until she's finished. With luck I'll get there in time for the dinner and nobody will notice that I missed the lecture.' She took a battered packet of Carroll's from the pocket of her white coat.

'I thought you were trying to stop smoking,' Barry reproached her, but automatically reached into his pocket for a box of matches.

'I can't pretend to be sorry that I'm missing Conor's dreary old lecture.' She ignored his stricture and leaned forward to let him light her cigarette.

Barry extracted a pipe from the litter of papers on the desk and tried to use the same match to light it. 'I have to wait for a student too. Peter McCormack is so far behind with his project that I hadn't the heart to send him home.' His pipe hadn't caught and the flame was burning his fingers. He shook out the match angrily and lit another one. 'I could keep an eye on Maeve for you,' he mumbled as he sucked the flame down into the pipe. 'You

9

might still catch the end of the lecture.' He looked at his watch. 'It's only half past seven.'

'Thanks, but no thanks.' She stepped into the room and closed the door. 'I'd prefer to take this chance to have a word with you. I never seem to see you lately.'

'I'm very busy,' Barry protested, but she was already clearing a pile of essays off the spare chair and drawing it up beside him.

'What are you doing?' She peered over his shoulder.

He picked up the papers he'd been working on and shoved them into his briefcase. 'Just making a few notes from some old articles — for the introduction to a paper I'm writing.'

'What about my manuscript?' She inhaled sharply on her cigarette. 'It's been sitting here since Christmas. You claim you haven't time to read it but you can find time to write a paper of your own.'

'I've read it but I haven't had enough time to think about it.' He seemed anxious to placate her. 'Could we talk about it tomorrow?'

'There's nothing to talk about; it's not controversial. Why don't we just submit it and let the editors decide whether it's publishable?'

'I'd rather we didn't do that,' he said with an air of finality and looked round as if for some avenue of escape. 'I haven't got time to discuss this now. I have a lot of things on my mind.'

'This is a wonderful collaboration. I spend hours writing a paper that you haven't time to read properly, yet I come in here and find you working on another paper that you won't even let me see.' She reached for the ashtray and viciously stubbed out her cigarette.

'You'll see it soon enough,' he said quietly, not reacting to her anger. 'Now, if you're not going to the lecture shouldn't you be keeping an eye on your student?'

The legs of her chair rasped against the tiles as she stood up and wrenched open the door. 'You'd better find time tomorrow to discuss that paper.' She pulled the door closed again and stood with her back to it. 'I did all the work.' Her voice rose with frustration. 'I'll publish it on my own if you go on like this. Don't worry, your contribution will be acknowledged in a footnote. You've been so difficult to talk to recently that even that will be more than you deserve.'

*   *   *

'In conclusion, ladies and gentlemen, you must forgive me if I ride one of my favourite hobbyhorses. Many lay people, and, regrettably, many molecular biologists, believe that the science of genetics is an invention of the 1980s. While it must be admitted that many of the recent developments in the technology of genetic manipulation have indeed permitted quite, eh ... dramatic advances in our knowledge of the principles of inheritance, I would urge the younger scientists among you not to ignore the pioneering work carried out when genetics was, as Myles na gCopaleen would say, "neither popular nor profitable". I hope in tonight's lecture I have been able to show, in my own small way, that work I began a quarter of a century ago still has significance in the context of modern molecular genetics.'

As the applause died away, Robert Roche, in the chair, formally thanked the speaker and rapidly brought the proceedings to a conclusion. 'Splendid lecture,' he congratulated Conor Dodd fulsomely and shook his hand. In a conspiratorial whisper, made unnecessary by the noise of the audience leaving the hall, he added, 'I must say I enjoyed your parting shot over the bows of the young tigers. I look forward to hearing how Brian and Catherine react to your remarks.'

11

'I didn't intend to give the impression of a personal attack on anybody.' Dodd was fussing with his lecture notes. 'I tease Catherine about her "Third Industrial Revolution" but I hope nobody thought I was getting at her or Brian. I must make a point of seeing them during the reception.'

'Speaking of which, let's go and get some sherry.' Roche took him firmly by the elbow and ushered him off the podium. 'You've earned a drink after your brilliant exegesis.'

'I'd love a sherry,' Dodd agreed as Roche piloted him deftly across the crowded lobby towards a waiter. 'Your health, Bob, and thank you for your flattering introduction to my little talk. You made me feel quite important.'

Roche was peering around in desperation. 'There are Paul and Colette, looking a bit lost. Excuse me, old chap.' He patted Dodd's arm absently. 'I must go and introduce them to a few people.'

Dodd seemed equally relieved to be spared more bonhomie. 'I must find Catherine and Brian and make sure they took no offence at my remarks,' he murmured at Roche's retreating back.

* * *

Mitchell had drunk three cups of tea and read every bit of his *Evening Herald*. The nine o'clock news was nearly over and he really should be going for that walk. While he was lacing his shoes, the weather forecaster was predicting 'squally showers' for the Dublin area. Should he just walk as far as Lynch's, have the couple of pints and get an early night? If it was going to rain, maybe he'd better take the car after all. Searching for his keys, he heard the phone ring. It was probably for one of the young women in the flat downstairs, but they were on night duty this week. He found his keys in the kitchenette and the phone was still ringing. He took his time going downstairs, glaring at the phone, willing it to stop.

'Mitch?' He recognised Donal O'Loughlin's brisk Donegal accent and wished he'd walked past the phone. 'I'm glad I caught you, I was afraid you'd be gone out. Get out to the university, as quick as you can. There's been a shooting incident there and the local station has asked for assistance. I know you're supposed to be off tonight,' O'Loughlin forestalled his protests, 'but if this turns out to be something serious, you'll have to take charge and you'd best be there from the outset. I can't see myself finished with this wretched court case before the end of next week.'

'Bloody students! I wouldn't mind shooting a few of them myself.'

'Restrain yourself, Mitch. I believe the victim is one of the staff, and it sounds as if he shot himself.'

'Sorry, sir.' Mitchell was sobered. He dreaded suicide cases, with all their attendant euphemisms and prevarication. 'Where exactly did the incident happen? It's a big place, I'd better know where I'm going.'

'In the Genetics Department, which is in the O'Meara Building. You'll find Superintendent McGrath there. I've already dispatched Sergeant Smith with a technical team and Bangharda Brennan is at home if you need her.'

'Right, sir. I'll be there right away. With any luck we'll be able to wrap it up before midnight.'

2

He had no difficulty identifying the O'Meara Building. Like the other college buildings, it was a three-storey structure of concrete and glass. Its designer had departed from the conventional cube and the two wings of the building converged at an obtuse angle, in the apex of which shallow steps led up to the main door. Clustered in the forecourt, Mitchell counted three patrol cars, two motorcycles and an ambulance. Any hope of maintaining discretion about the shooting could be forgotten.

In the entrance hall Sam Smith was taking notes while he chatted to a uniformed superintendent. The sergeant introduced Mitchell to the senior officer.

'You got here quickly, inspector.' The superintendent sounded relieved and he put on his cap in anticipation of imminent departure. 'I've told the sergeant all I know about the circumstances. It's probably suicide, but I'd like you lads to have a look, just to be on the safe side. The deceased is Professor Brian Barry, God rest his soul. A colleague found him lying dead in his office with a revolver in his hand. A local doctor has verified death. Apart from that, nothing has been touched.'

He edged towards the door. 'If you're happy to take over here, inspector, I'll leave you to it. I still have one or two things to do before finishing up.'

One or two pints more likely, Mitchell thought enviously, as the superintendent climbed into the back of one of the patrol cars.

Mitchell was watching Sam with silent amusement. The sergeant hated standing around doing nothing, but knew better than to let anybody near the scene of crime before Mitchell arrived. He knew Sam didn't believe his claim to be able to learn more by taking a good hard look for five minutes than the Technical Bureau, with their tapes and test tubes, could discover in a week. Mitchell could still remember the dressing down he'd given Sam five years ago, during the first murder case they'd worked on together. Arriving at the scene of crime to find all the furniture moved and the victim surrounded by chalk marks and print powder, he'd said some hard things. Sam had seen the point when the case was eventually thrown out of court for lack of evidence.

'It's on the first floor, sir.' Smith led the way up a steep flight of stairs and along a narrow corridor. The rooms on both sides were in darkness but they could hear the intermittent hum of electric motors, and here and there the glow of a pilot light was visible through glass panels in the doors. 'These are all laboratories and instrument rooms, sir,' the sergeant explained. 'The staff have their offices leading off the labs.'

An open door at the end of the corridor led into a brightly lit laboratory. The room was tidy, but every shelf was crammed with bottles and jars of reagents and the benches were covered with beakers and flasks. Most of the floor space between the benches was taken up by equipment of various sorts: a glass-topped cabinet in which flasks with white cotton-wool bungs moved in endless whirling circles, a grey metal console on which digits flashed silently on and off. On a shelf above the

15

sink a complicated glass still steamed and bubbled. Mitchell sniffed in an effort to identify the pungent mixture of smells that permeated the room. The odours of captans and acetic acid were familiar from his school days, but other, more exotic elements eluded him. Smith indicated a door in the far corner of the laboratory. 'That's Professor Barry's office, sir.'

Mitchell stood in the doorway and surveyed the cluttered room. The wall facing him was lined with shelves of books. Below these, files and journals were stacked on a bench that ran the length of the office. On Mitchell's right, a built-in desk occupied the space beneath a large window. Seated in front of the desk, chest and arms slumped over the papers on its surface, was the body of a small, wiry man. His head was resting on the crook of the left elbow, and his fine sandy hair had fallen forward so that it almost obscured the bullet wound just above the right eye. The other arm was extended towards Mitchell as if reaching for the revolver that lay on the desk beneath the fingertips of the right hand.

After more than twenty years as a policeman, Mitchell wasn't squeamish about corpses, but he'd never quite got over a feeling of diffidence in the presence of death. He was embarrassed by the crassness of his intrusion into the silence and privacy of death; even death by violence brought stillness and peace after the event.

He studied the scene silently for some minutes before taking out his notebook and making a list of the objects on the desk: a cardboard box filled with letters and circulars, a pile of books, half-a-dozen journals with coloured covers, two metal file-boxes, a stack of notepaper bearing the college coat of arms, two pencils and an open fountain pen, an ancient penknife lying on top of a tin of tobacco, and a brass ashtray containing a single cigarette stub and several burnt-out matches.

16

'All right, Sam, you can let the technical lads loose, and the pathologist can go ahead as soon as he arrives. It certainly looks like suicide but make sure the room gets the full treatment.' Mitchell prowled around the laboratory but he didn't know anything about genetics, so it told him very little. He peered out one of the windows. A small crowd of onlookers had gathered outside, but a couple of uniformed gardai were keeping them at bay.

'Were there any witnesses?'

'There were five people in the building when the local guards arrived, sir. They're in the common room on the ground floor.'

* * *

The atmosphere of scholarly comfort in the common room was in sharp contrast to the spartan clutter of the laboratories. Two sides of the room were dominated by large windows, now almost hidden behind heavy curtains of red velvet which complemented the rich brown of polished teak floor, tables and the bookshelves that lined the two remaining walls.

Three young men and a young woman were sitting at one of the tables. The woman had obviously been crying and the men looked scarcely more composed. At the other side of the room a tall woman in a white coat was standing at a trolley, spooning instant coffee into a row of mugs. She looked remote and clinical in her starched coat, with her dark hair pinned smoothly back on the nape of her neck. Her neat movements seemed out of tune with the emotional tension in the room.

Mitchell introduced himself. 'I'll need a statement from everybody who was in the building when the shooting occurred.' He addressed a stocky bearded man, probably in his late twenties, who looked the oldest of the group at the table. The man looked rather helplessly at

17

his companions before turning for guidance to the woman at the trolley. She had put down the tin of coffee and was studying Mitchell. He felt he was being expertly appraised and not meeting some unspecified standard. She picked up a tea-towel and wiped her hands.

'I'd better make the introductions,' she said as she walked towards them. Unconsciously Mitchell registered her legs, long and slim in dark tights and black high-heeled shoes. 'I'm Catherine Gildea and this is David Morgan.' The bearded man stood up and shook hands heartily with the inspector. She turned to the other three at the table, 'These are Owen O'Neill, Peter McCormack and Maeve Carty. We were all in the building when the shooting occurred.'

'You all work here?' Mitchell asked, as he jotted down the names in his notebook.

'Dr Morgan and I are on the staff, and Owen is a post-graduate student. Maeve and Peter are undergraduates in their final year.'

To Mitchell's dismay, Maeve Carty, at the mention of her name, or perhaps at the sight of the notebook, started to sob noisily, and Owen O'Neill, sitting beside her, put an arm protectively around her shoulder. David Morgan, on her other side, looked embarrassed but patted her hand.

'For heaven's sake pull yourself together and stop crying.' Gildea took a clean handkerchief from her pocket and handed it to Maeve. 'Please sit down, inspector.' She indicated a chair at the other end of the table. 'There'll be coffee as soon as the kettle boils.'

Mitchell turned again to David Morgan. 'Perhaps, sir, you would start by telling me exactly what happened here tonight.'

'Catherine will tell you.' There was a musical lilt in Morgan's speech. Mitchell realised that he was probably

18

Welsh, which might explain his reluctance to become involved with the Irish police.

The inspector sat with his notebook open on the table in front of him and watched Gildea dispensing coffee. Her gestures were deft and precise as she moved between the trolley and the table. She was the sort of woman he liked least: self-possessed, efficient and cold.

'Now, Miss Gildea, what happened tonight?'

'I was working in my room, which is on the second floor, directly above Professor Barry's.' She picked up a mug of coffee and sat down opposite Mitchell. 'At about half past eight I heard a loud bang. I thought it came from the basement where Owen and Maeve were working, so I went down there in the lift, but everything was all right. I knew Professor Barry had been in his room earlier this evening, so I went to ask if he had heard anything.'

Her voice faltered. She drank some coffee which seemed to steady her. 'He was slumped over his desk with a gun in his hand. I tried to find his pulse but could feel nothing, so I used his phone to call our security office and asked them to ring the police and an ambulance. Then I went back to the basement to tell the students what had happened. Maeve got rather upset so we brought her back up to my office, and Owen and I went together through both wings of the building to see if there was anybody else around.'

Mitchell laid down his pen and drank his coffee, watching Catherine Gildea over the rim of his mug. She was undoubtedly handsome, with good bone structure and fine skin, but there was a hardness in her expression and a coldness in the blue eyes that he found disconcerting.

'The only people we found were Dr Morgan, who was in his room in the other wing, and Peter, who was in one of the laboratories over there. Owen went and collected

19

Maeve and we all waited here until the police arrived.'

Mitchell realised that, while he had been studying her, Gildea had concluded her story and was expecting him to respond. 'That's very concise,' he said hurriedly. 'Could you be more specific about the noise you heard?'

'Not really.' She shook her head. 'It was just a loud thump. It must have been the shot, but at the time I was sure it was the cell disintegrator in the basement. It's been giving trouble recently. It works under very high pressure and I thought the damn thing had finally disintegrated itself, to tell you the truth.' Mitchell thought she giggled, but it might have been only a sharp intake of breath.

'This was about half past eight?' Mitchell glanced back through his notes. 'Are you sure about the time?'

'I didn't look at my watch when I heard the bang but it was eight forty-two when I phoned security. No more than five or six minutes had elapsed after the shot.'

Mitchell turned abruptly to her colleague. 'Can you add anything to Miss Gildea's statement, Dr Morgan?'

'No, I'm afraid not, inspector. My room is in the other wing. I heard nothing and wasn't aware of anything amiss until Owen and Catherine arrived at my office.'

'What did you do then?'

'I helped them look around the remainder of the west wing but Peter was the only other person there. We just came back here and waited for the police.'

'Are there usually so many people here at that hour of the evening?'

'Oh, yes, inspector.' Morgan seemed more expansive on this topic. 'Genetics isn't a nine-to-five job. Microorganisms, you know, don't always grow fast enough for us to finish an experiment and get home in time for tea.'

Mitchell nodded absently and turned to the students who had been listening in silence to the proceedings. 'Is there anything you'd like to add?'

Owen put his arm around Maeve again and answered for them both. 'No, inspector. Maeve and I were together in the basement all the time. We didn't hear anything unusual but the disintegrator is very noisy and we were wearing earmuffs, so we didn't even hear the lift when Catherine came down.'

'I didn't hear anything either,' Peter McCormack chimed in. 'I was in the other wing all evening.'

Mitchell jotted, 'McCormack — over-anxious?' before closing his notebook and slipping it into his pocket. 'You youngsters can go home now, but we'll probably want you to make statements tomorrow.'

Catherine Gildea stood up and began to collect the mugs onto a tray. Mitchell lit a cigarette. 'Now, Dr Morgan, what can you tell me about Professor Barry?'

'Not very much, inspector. I only came here from Cardiff at Christmas. Catherine would know him much better than I do.'

'Well, Miss Gildea, you seem to have a monopoly on information around here.' Mitchell sighed audibly.

She put down the tray. 'Professor Barry was an associate professor. He was on the staff here for nearly twenty years. He was forty-four years of age, married, with four children.' Her voice sounded wooden, as if she was reciting a passage learnt by heart.

'When did you last see him alive?'

'I was talking to him at about half past seven, just after I came back from my tea. I was surprised to see a light in his room, so I looked in to see if he was there.' She picked up the tray and carried it to a sink in the corner. 'He was busy so I didn't stay long,' she added with her back to the inspector.

'Why were you surprised to find him here?' Mitchell turned his chair around so that he could see her. 'I under-

21

stood from Dr Morgan that people are often here at that hour.'

She ran hot water into a plastic bowl and started to wash the mugs, talking to Mitchell over her shoulder. 'Tonight is exceptional, inspector. All the staff were invited to a special meeting of the Science Institute at the Burlington Hotel. Brian was on the council of the Institute this year, so I assumed he would be at the meeting. However, he said he had a student to supervise and was too busy to go.'

'What was the special occasion?' Mitchell got up from the table and stationed himself near the sink, where he could see her face. Her cheeks were flushed, possibly from the hot water.

'The Institute is celebrating its centenary. We were all invited because one of our colleagues, Professor Dodd, is being presented with the Institute medal and is giving the celebratory address.'

'Why are you and Dr Morgan not at the meeting?'

'I had hoped to attend, but at the last moment I found that I had to stay here because Maeve wanted to finish some experiments.' She picked up a tea-towel and began to dry the mugs. 'Because of insurance problems, there's a rule that undergraduates may not be in the laboratories after six o'clock unless there is a member of staff present. I hoped to get to the Burlington later in the evening.'

'And you, Dr Morgan?' The Welshman had joined him beside the sink.

'Professor Dodd was kind enough to invite me but I wanted to work. I have a lot of classes to prepare and I couldn't really afford to take a night off.'

'When you were talking to Professor Barry, Miss Gildea, what state of mind was he in?' She had moved back to the trolley and both men followed her. 'Did he strike you as being depressed in any way?'

'Not depressed, but he seemed a bit uneasy.' She wiped the surface thoroughly and arranged the clean mugs in a tidy row.

'What do you mean by "uneasy"?'

'He seemed under pressure, almost nervous. I got the distinct impression that he wanted me to go away. He told me several times how busy he was.'

'What did you talk about?'

'Nothing very much, really.' She took a battered packet of cigarettes from her pocket and, sitting down again at the table, lit one with a slim gold lighter. 'Each of us explained why we weren't at the Burlington. Then we talked briefly about a project we're collaborating on, but because he was busy I didn't delay for more than a few minutes.'

'You have no idea why he shot himself?'

'You're sure it was suicide?'

'You saw the body yourself, Miss Gildea.' He sat down opposite her again. 'Can you think of any reason why he might have committed suicide?'

'I can't imagine him having a gun, let alone shooting himself or anybody else.'

'Don't forget that several hundred people in this country kill themselves every year, notwithstanding the reluctance of Irish juries to bring in a suicide verdict. Very few of them are the so-called "suicidal types".' He looked across the table at her but she was staring at her left hand which was playing restlessly with her lighter. Her fingers were long and shapely and he noticed that she wore no rings. 'When I've made a complete forensic examination, I'll be able to tell you whether it was suicide.' He stood up. 'In the meantime you can both go home. I'll talk to you again tomorrow.'

'I'd like to call the Burlington before I leave.' Gildea

took a telephone directory from one of the shelves. 'I'd better tell our head of department about Brian. I'd have phoned him earlier but I didn't like to do it until somebody had broken the news to Anna Barry. Has anybody been in touch with her yet, inspector?'

'No, that's my job. I'll go and do it now if you can tell me where she lives.'

'In Sandymount.' Gildea had picked up a phone and was trying to get an outside line. 'Break it to her gently. It will be a dreadful shock for her. Tell her to phone me at home if there is anything I can do to help.'

'If you know Mrs Barry well, Miss Gildea,' Mitchell had a sudden inspiration, 'perhaps you'd like to come with me. It might help her to have somebody she knows there.'

She put down the receiver. The suggestion was obviously a shock, but she nodded acquiescence.

'There are one or two things I need to do before we go,' Mitchell said as he headed for the door. 'Make your phone call and I'll meet you in the hall here in ten minutes.'

*　*　*

Maurice Keane, his shirt sleeves rolled back to the elbows, was washing his hands at the sink in Barry's laboratory.

'Anything for me?

'Very little.' The pathologist continued to scrub his nails methodically, but peered over his spectacles at Mitchell. 'He's dead, but he hasn't been dead for very long — not more than two hours, I'd say.'

'Suicide?'

'Maybe.' Keane had finished scrubbing his hands and was looking around for a towel. 'Maybe not.'

Mitchell found a roll of paper towels on one of the

benches and handed it to him.

'I hope your technical people can come up with an opinion one way or the other,' Keane said, as he dried his hands and adjusted the cuffs of his shirt. 'I've only had a superficial look at the body. I'll do a full autopsy tomorrow morning, but I suspect that my report will be inconclusive.' He shrugged on an ancient tweed jacket and picked up his bag. 'What do you think, yourself, Mitch?'

'Looks like suicide, certainly.' Mitchell wandered over to inspect the scene again. 'But it's almost too neat, too tidy.'

Sam Smith was in the office. 'We're finished here, sir. Can I let them take his nibs away?'

Mitchell watched the ambulance crew ease the body away from the desk. 'Hold it a second, lads. What's that under the left hand?'

Gently, using a paper towel, he lifted a pipe away from the stiffening fingers. 'Maurice, did you see this?' He bent to examine the corpse more closely. 'There are scorch marks on his tie where the pipe was pressed against it.' He stood back to let the pathologist get a better view. 'Have you ever come across anybody committing suicide with a pipe in one hand and a gun in the other?'

'Professionally, I regard all smokers as suicides.' Keane took a lens from his breast pocket and examined the left hand minutely. 'However, I agree it's unusual to be smoking as you pull the trigger.'

25

3

Mitchell saw her as he ran down the stairs. She was standing absolutely still, watching as the plastic bag containing Barry's remains was carried on a stretcher through the hall. Now wearing a scarlet anorak and flat-heeled shoes, she looked smaller, younger and very vulnerable. It had been stupid to tell her to wait for him there. He could have spared her the body bag.

She said nothing but fell into step with him as he crossed the hall to the front door. It was raining heavily and he ran down the steps ahead of her to open the car door.

'Thank you for coming with me,' he said as he got into the car beside her. 'I've arranged for a bangharda to meet us at the house but it will be easier for Mrs Barry and, to be honest, easier for me if you're there.'

'You didn't give me much choice, inspector.' Her seat-belt caught on its roller and she tugged at it angrily. It was the first emotion she had shown all evening; but, as if exhausted by her brief display of temper, she relapsed into silence. As he turned into the main road, Mitchell glanced at her. She was staring fixedly at the windscreen, but as they passed under a lamp-post the light was reflected by tears running down her cheek. She wasn't sniffing or sobbing. She simply sat there, making no attempt to hide her tears or to wipe them away.

'Would you like me to pull in for a while?' His question disrupted her trance-like state and she rubbed her eyes, like a child, with the back of her hand. He pulled the car off the road and, without comment, lit two cigarettes and handed her one.

'I'm sorry.' She leaned back against the head-rest and drew gratefully on the cigarette. 'I'll be all right in a minute. I won't be much help to Anna if I arrive in this state.'

'There's a box of tissues under the seat.'

They sat and smoked in silence. The rain was beating on the roof of the car and running in rivulets down the windscreen. Sheets of water broke against the door as the traffic sped past.

'Poor little Maeve, if she could see me now!' Gildea said suddenly and made a rueful sound halfway between a giggle and a sob.

'You were a bit hard on her.' He rubbed the windscreen with the side of his hand to clear the condensation, and studiously avoided looking at her. 'She's very young.'

'Yes, I could see you thought I was a bitch.' She said it without rancour. 'But I had to get her to stop crying. One more sniff out of her and I would have broken down there and then.'

'Would that have been so bad?'

'For God's sake, somebody had to cope.' She sounded more sure of herself. 'I was the most senior person there. It had to be me.' She ground her cigarette briskly in the ashtray. 'I thought I was going to be all right until I saw that wretched plastic bag.'

'I'm sorry.' He turned towards her but her face was hidden by a handful of tissues. 'That was my fault.'

'They had to take him away sometime.'

'I told the lads that everybody had left. I forgot you were waiting for me in the hall.'

'Oh, I'd have broken down sooner or later. It's probably just as well to get the tears over before I see Anna.' She rummaged in her handbag and produced some make-up. 'We'd better be on our way. I can repair my face as we go.'

He started the engine and eased the car back into the traffic. 'Tell me about Barry's family.'

'There are four children. They're quite young. I think the eldest is fifteen.'

'And Mrs Barry, what's she like?'

'Anna is great. She's from Yorkshire. She was a physiotherapist in the hospital in London where Brian did his PhD. But she's thoroughly acclimatised and is very involved in community groups and local politics.'

'What about other family: parents, brothers or sisters?'

'Brian's mother has lived with them since she was widowed a few years ago. Brian had several brothers and sisters but I think most of them live abroad. I only know one of his brothers, the awful Sean.'

'Sean Barry — why do I know that name?'

'You want the next turn left, then it's the third house on your right.'

Mitchell noticed with relief that the lights were still on in the house. At least they wouldn't have to waken the household. He parked and switched off the engine.

Gildea showed no inclination to get out of the car. 'Sean Barry is a self-styled man of letters. He writes "thought-provoking" pieces in the less discriminating rags. He's better known for his extreme nationalist opinions than for any literary talent.' Contempt made her sound almost cheerful.

'Did his brother share his political views?'

'Not at all. Even back in the early seventies, when it

was still fashionable to harbour republican aspirations, Brian took his brother quite publicly to task. He wrote some scathing letters to *The Irish Times*, denouncing Sean's ambivalence towards murder and violence.'

'You sound more robust.' He opened the door, 'Come on, we'd better get this over with.'

* * *

'I never, never want to see that happen to anybody again.' Catherine Gildea said through clenched teeth. 'Imagine coming back from a pleasant evening at the bridge club to face that news.' She lit a cigarette and inhaled deeply. 'There can be no easy way of hearing that your husband is dead, but I must say you broke the news as gently as possible. Do they train you for that sort of thing?'

'Only what you might call on-the-job training, watching senior officers do it. We get more practice than you might imagine. It's not just murder and suicide, mostly it's accidents: motor crashes and industrial accidents. Those are often the worst. Losing the breadwinner can be a terrible blow to a working-class family. At least Mrs Barry won't have financial worries. The college would have a good pension plan.'

'Money would be the last thing a woman would think about at a time like this,' she objected austerely.

'If most of your furniture is on HP and all you've got to fall back on is social welfare, you think about it pretty fast.'

She seemed cowed by his rebuke and relapsed into silence. He hoped fervently that she wouldn't break into tears again. 'Where do you live yourself?' he asked, glad of something to say. 'I'll drop you home.'

She was still subdued but, to his relief, her voice was steady. 'On Londonbridge Avenue, but if you're going back to the college, I'd like to get my car.'

'You're not in any state to be driving.' He looked sideways at her. She was huddled into her anorak. Cigarette ash had fallen on her skirt, but she seemed to lack the energy to brush it off. 'You needn't be worrying about the car, the place will be crawling with gardai tonight.'

Mitchell parked outside her house but she made no move to get out of the car. 'I'll see you to your door,' he prompted her.

'Don't you want another statement from me tonight?' She sounded weary.

'No, I only said that in case you felt you should offer to stay with Mrs Barry. You've had enough for one day.'

She looked up at him in surprise. 'Thank you.' She picked up her handbag and fumbled at the catch on the door. 'I'd ask you in for a drink but I suppose you're still on duty.'

'No, I'm finished for the night now.' Her offer hadn't sounded very enthusiastic but he was dying for a drink. It was almost midnight and in his absence the law-abiding Paddy Lynch would have shown the last customer off his premises half an hour ago. 'A drink would be very welcome, if it's not too much trouble. But just the one, mind.'

He could have guessed she'd live in a house like this. Small, but probably expensive in this part of the city, in a two-storeyed red-brick terrace, mid-nineteenth-century — the genuine article, not a modern imitation — the front door characteristically on the upper floor.

At the top of the steps, he rested one foot on the cast-iron boot-scraper while she fumbled in her pockets for the key. He was getting very wet and wished she'd hurry up. Having finally found the key and unlocked the door, she delayed again with her hand on an inner glass-panelled door.

'Come in and shut the door behind you. The beasts are poised to attack as soon as I open this.'

For a moment he was afraid that the trauma of the evening had unhinged the woman's mind, but when she opened the door an avalanche of black fur poured through it and two glistening black cats proceeded to rub themselves into an ecstasy of purring against both pairs of ankles.

'I'm sorry about this.' She took his anorak and hung it with her own on the hall stand. 'Meet Watson and Crick. They're not always so demanding, but their supper is several hours overdue. However, I'm sure your need is greater than theirs. Come into the sitting-room and I'll get you a drink.'

She threaded her way through the cats into the front room where she opened the door of an old-fashioned sideboard. 'You'll have a drop of whiskey?'

She moved a small step up in Mitchell's estimation by producing a bottle of Crested Ten. 'Thanks. That's my favourite whiskey — but just a small one.'

She was decent enough not to take him at his word, but poured a generous measure of whiskey into a Waterford tumbler. She seemed flustered, and fussed unnecessarily about getting a small table to put beside him and a coaster for his drink. He wondered if it was an unusual experience for her to have a man in the house at this hour of the night.

The room faced west and the rain was being blown with force against the sash-window, causing the panes to rattle. She shivered as she closed the shutters and drew the curtains. 'Horrible night!

He sipped his drink and examined his surroundings while his hostess retired to the kitchen to feed the cats. Though the room was warm and comfortable, it lacked personality. It was too tidy: the books neatly shelved, the chairs arranged at symmetrical angles to the fireplace. No clutter, no out-of-date newspapers or half-eaten bars of chocolate. It reminded him of the parlour in his mother's house, never used except for visitors.

'Was this your family home?' he asked as she came back into the room and poured a whiskey for herself. He noticed that she was equally generous with her own drink.

'No, I'm a runner-in, like yourself, but I hadn't far to come. My family lives in Dalkey, but I wanted a place of my own.' She had evidently decided to light a fire and was cutting open a bail of turf. 'You're from a lot farther south than that?'

Before he could reply, she pointed the scissors at him accusingly. 'Don't ask me why I think so. You'll only prove that you're a Kerryman, living up to your reputation of answering every question with another question.'

He laughed, curiously pleased that she was pulling his leg. 'Guilty as charged, Dr Gildea. I'm from just outside Glenbeigh.'

'Please, Inspector Mitchell, now that you've finally brought yourself to address me as "doctor", could I persuade you to call me Catherine instead?' She said it lightly, but there was an edge of derision in her voice.

Mitchell blushed. 'I hoped you mightn't have registered that little piece of bad manners. If I apologise, will you take into account my other offences of the evening?' He realised this sounded glib and decided to be honest. 'My first impressions of you were wrong. You seemed stuck-up and heartless, and I suppose I was trying to take you down a peg. I'm sorry.'

He stood up and held out his hand to her. 'By the same token, my first name is Michael but my friends call me Mitch.'

She took his hand but was obviously embarrassed and

said hurriedly, 'You'd better have another drink. If you start being nice to me I'll probably begin weeping again.'

She ignored his half-hearted refusal and refilled his glass. They sipped their drinks in silence and Mitchell was in no hurry to break it. He wanted her to do the talking.

'You told Anna that Brian's death was accidental,' she said eventually. 'Is that a possibility?'

'Probably not.' He shrugged. 'However, we'll let Mrs Barry work that out for herself when she gets over the shock and thinks rationally about the circumstances. In the meantime, it's an easier idea to confront than suicide.'

The fire was blazing nicely and she sat on a stool beside it, thinking about the implications of this answer. 'I can't accept that Brian killed himself.' She put up a hand to forestall any comment. 'It's not just a feeling that it wouldn't be in character. There was something wrong about the way he looked.' She frowned in concentration, but finally shook her head. 'Maybe I'll remember to-morrow when my mind is clearer. I don't want to think about it any more tonight.' She took a large gulp of whiskey as if to dispel unwelcome images.

'I can show you photographs tomorrow; they might jog your memory.' She expressed no enthusiasm for this suggestion and he decided to level with her in the hope of drawing her out. 'You might be right. One bit of evidence supports your view: Barry seems to have had a lighted pipe in his hand when he died. I can't see anybody going to the trouble of lighting a pipe and then, just when it was drawing nicely, blowing his brains out.'

'Oh, it was a departmental joke: that Brian would die with that awful pipe in his mouth.' She gave a sickly grin. 'Seriously, that makes the idea of suicide even more unconvincing. I can't see Brian with his pipe in one hand and a gun in the other.' She caught her breath abruptly and Mitchell was afraid she was about to break into tears again. 'Wait a minute, that's it! His pipe in his left hand and the gun in his right!' she repeated slowly with appropriate gestures. 'Doesn't that suggest anything to you?'

He shook his head blankly.

'Do you smoke a pipe yourself?'

'Occasionally. I'm trying to cut down on the cigarettes.'

'Have you got it there? Take it out and put it into your mouth.' She sounded excited, and watched carefully as he obeyed. 'You're right-handed. Brian was left-handed, that's why the pipe was in his left hand. He wouldn't have used a gun with his right hand.'

'Are you sure he was a *ciotóg*?'

'I'm certain, but not everybody might have realised it.' She spoke animatedly, leaning forward, willing Mitchell to believe her. 'As a youngster he was taught to write with his right hand but he used his left hand for everything else. He played squash as a left-hander, and if you look in his desk you should find a pair of left-handed scissors which I bought him in London. He was always complaining that he couldn't cut his fingernails.'

'That's interesting.' Mitchell was not prepared to commit himself. He put the pipe back into his pocket and took out a packet of cigarettes.

'I want to believe that Brian didn't kill himself.' She accepted a cigarette and her eyes pleaded with Mitchell for reassurance as he lit it for her. When he refused to respond, she eventually admitted, 'I don't suppose the alternative idea is very palatable either.'

'Was Brian Barry a close friend as well as being your boss?'

'He wasn't my *boss*.' She sounded quite annoyed by the suggestion. 'He was senior to me. I consulted him about my work and I did what he suggested a lot of the time, but only because I respected his judgement.'

'But you were friends?'

'Yes, we were friends. I was Brian's postgraduate student, so we've known each other a long time. He and Anna were among my closest friends.'

'Just supposing he was murdered, can you think of anybody who hated, or feared, him enough to kill him?'

She tapped cigarette ash thoughtfully into the fire. 'I can't truthfully say Brian had no enemies. In fact he was rather good at making enemies. Academic life is full of hypocrisy and cant, and he always felt obliged to expose them, even on occasions when he would have done better to keep his mouth shut. However, in recent years he seemed to have given up the unequal struggle.' She shook her head confidently. 'I don't believe he had any current enemies.'

'Tell me about your colleagues. Who else works in the department?'

She counted on her fingers. 'There are nine of us on the teaching staff. Bob Roche is the head of department. He's a full professor. Then there are, or were, two associate professors, Brian and Conor Dodd. Pat McIvor and I are senior lecturers. Pat is on sabbatical, he's been in Vancouver since January.'

'You don't look like a senior anything.' Mitchell was genuinely surprised.

'I'm thirty-nine,' she protested with candour. 'They promote you after twelve years of faithful service, unless you're a real waster. I made the grade last year.'

'In mitigation of my earlier attitude, I thought you were still in your twenties.'

She brushed the compliment aside. 'Academics always look well-preserved. It's probably because we're with young people so much.'

'That should have quite the opposite effect and be a cause for grey hairs.' Unconsciously, he ran his fingers through his own hair. 'I interrupted you. Who else is on the staff?'

'There's David Morgan, who's on the bottom rung of the ladder. Paul Mooney and Colette Lalor have both been on the staff for about five years and Chris O'Mahony has been around for as long as myself.'

'And you're all one big happy family?'

'Nobody loves an informer,' she reproved him, and examined the contents of her glass for a moment before continuing. 'I suppose you want to know about the undercurrents. She pointed at the whiskey bottle. 'Help yourself.' She seemed deep in concentration. 'This may take some time. Like any divided community, you need a knowledge of our history before you can understand the tensions.

He didn't even make a pretence of refusing another drink. She waited until he had refilled both glasses, before she began. 'As they'd say in your part of the country, *"bhí fear ann fadó"* — old Professor O'Meara, who was a genius but quite mad. He quarrelled with everybody in the college except his own staff and students, but we idolised him. The department was very small in those days. Bob Roche seemed an old man to me when I was a student, but he can only have been in his early forties, not much older than I am now. Conor Dodd and Brian were bright young men. Brian had just finished his doctorate in London and was an assistant lecturer grade nothing. I was supposed to be doing my PhD with O'Meara but in practice Brian supervised me. He was the only one who took the trouble to teach me anything and to make sure I did a bit of work.'

She paused to light a cigarette. 'I wasn't a very dedicated scientist in those days.' She sounded almost wistful. 'I had too many other interests, I suppose. Brian was a perfectionist and a hard taskmaster. I was much more afraid of him than of the prof, who was a pet but, I can see now, was scandalously neglectful of his students.'

Mitchell was amused by her tone of indignation but she must have realised that she sounded pompous, because she giggled. 'He used to toddle into the lab every so often and ask me how I was getting on, then escape again as quickly as possible. I discovered years afterwards that he was always embarrassed because he could never remember my name.'

'But you still got the old PhD?'

'Only thanks to Brian.' The laughter left her voice and she sank again into contemplation of the fire.

'What happened next?' Mitchell was not prepared to let her indulge in self-pity.

'I went off to Yale.' She visibly pulled herself together. 'Doing my BTA.' She looked at him expectantly. 'Been To America,' she explained, when he failed to come in on cue: 'the mandatory qualification for any aspiring academic in those days.'

Mitchell laughed politely at the feeble joke, to encourage her to relax.

'The prof retired the following year and the bloodshed began. Bob Roche and Conor Dodd were both strong candidates for the chair and the appointment turned into a very bitter contest, the reverberations of which are still detectable in the department.' She looked questioningly at Mitchell as if to reassure herself of his interest.

'Go ahead,' he said noncommittally.

'In those days getting a chair was entirely a matter of canvassing. Academic appointments are made by the Senate, but the Faculty and the Academic Council also vote on the candidates. Most members of the Faculty would have some knowledge of the subject and of the candidates' abilities, but the Academic Council includes the professors from all faculties. The majority might

37

know nothing about the discipline in question. The same is true of the Senate which is a mixture of county councillors and academics.'

Mitchell couldn't resist interrupting her. 'You're using the present tense. Are appointments still made in this way?'

'Theoretically they are. The procedure is enshrined in statutes, but there is one important difference in the way things happen now. In recent years the candidates are interviewed and normally all the voting bodies accept the interview board's advice. It's unusual now for the recommended candidate not to get the job.' She paused to sip her drink before adding, 'It's taken a lot of the fun out of academic life.'

'Yes, I can see that it might. Is it any wonder universities are full of such oddball people — saving your presence, of course.'

She ignored him. 'Anyway, in 1970 we had Roche and Dodd keenly contesting the chair of genetics. There were other candidates of course but they were never really in the running. Of the two, Dodd had the edge academically. Although he was only in his thirties, he had published some very important papers. He won the vote at the Faculty by a respectable margin. Roche—another Kerryman, incidentally — was by far the more experienced politician. He must have done a whale of a canvass because he beat Dodd by a length at the Academic Council and ran away with the Senate.'

Watching her, Mitchell realised that, despite her overt disapproval of these political shenanigans, she enjoyed the frisson of academic intrigue. 'So Roche and Dodd have been deadly enemies ever since?' he prompted her.

She shook her head. 'It's not quite as simple as that. They're not exactly friends but they maintain a working relationship.'

'So what's the problem?'

'The real trouble with our appointment system is that it takes so long. In a tight contest everybody becomes involved, and feelings can be quite strong. Brian, as the youngest member of the staff, threw himself into the fray with all the subtlety of a young tiger and became unofficial election agent for Dodd.'

'Why?'

'I think he saw the contest as a cosmic struggle between scholarship and politics, with Dodd, an enthusiastic researcher, on the side of the angels. Incidentally,' she looked at Mitchell over the rim of her glass, 'it's something that Brian and I didn't see eye to eye about. I agree that Conor Dodd is a good scientist but I find him pompous and narcissistic. Bob, as long as he isn't expected to do any teaching, is easygoing and lets the rest of us get on with things. He's a better head of department than Conor would have been.'

Perhaps the whiskey was taking effect, or the shock was wearing off, but she seemed anxious to talk now. She got up and put more turf on the fire but continued to address Mitchell over her shoulder. 'We'll probably find out soon enough. Bob will be retiring within the next few years and I suppose Conor will get the chair. I had hoped it might have been Brian, but he always said he wouldn't run against Conor.'

'So there was no love lost between Brian Barry and Professor Roche?'

'That's about the size of it,' she agreed. 'It's funny, Roche seemed to focus his enmity on Brian rather than on Conor.' She brushed the hearth neatly. The turf dust ignited into a shower of sparks as she tossed it on the fire. 'I suppose it's a bit like a family quarrel. The principals may become reconciled, but God help the outsider who is foolish enough to take sides.'

'This was a long time ago,' Mitchell protested. 'Surely it doesn't affect the younger members of staff, such as yourself?'

'The bad feeling has been diluted as the department got bigger, but none of us has been entirely immune to it. For instance,' she sat down again and picked up her glass. 'Roche strongly opposed my appointment — partly because I was a protégée of Brian's, but also because a postgraduate student of his own was in the running. That dispute threatened to become so bitter that the college authorities, in their wisdom, agreed to appoint both of us. But Chris O'Mahony and I usually get on all right because he's good-natured and an extrovert. However, we tend to be perceived by others as being on opposite sides of an invisible divide. Much the same thing applies to Paul and Colette, but they've solved the problem by falling in love, and spend most of the time gazing into each other's eyes.'

'Are you suggesting that feelings are still strong enough to lead to murder?'

'No, of course not — at least I fervently hope not!' She laughed, but Mitchell could sense a tiny doubt developing in her mind. 'I was hesitant to say anything to you about the situation, in case you'd jump to that conclusion, but I was afraid you'd hear a more lurid version from somebody else.' She laughed again, nervously. 'Probably from the postgraduate students.'

'Don't tell me the situation affects them too?'

'Not at all,' she insisted, 'but they're terrible gossips, and the folklore passes from year to year and loses nothing in the telling. They're often better informed than the rest of us. They have a collective capacity for knowing what's going on, usually before it happens — and what they can't find out, they invent!'

She sipped her drink in silence for a few moments,

pondering the situation. 'Don't get the impression that we work in silent hostility. Superficially, relationships within the department are quite cordial. We go to each other's parties and so forth. The bad feeling exists only as *uisce faoi thalamh* — the undercurrents rarely surface.'

'If I'm not to find the murderer in your department, where else should I look? What about Barry's domestic life?'

'Brian was very happily married.' She stood up and rooted on the mantelpiece until she found a packet of cigarettes. 'Anna is marvellous. She has a strong personality and she's great fun. Brian needed somebody like that, he tended to take life rather too seriously.'

'What about another woman in Barry's life?' Mitchell asked as he stood up to light her cigarette.

She inhaled too quickly and the smoke made her cough.

'Come on, Catherine, you needn't pretend to be shocked,' he protested, as she stared coldly at him. 'Even university professors must occasionally have something on the side.'

'As far as I know there was nothing of that sort.' Sounding offended, she turned her back on him and walked across the room. He thought she was about to ask him to leave but she merely fetched an ashtray from the sideboard and came back to sit in an armchair opposite him. 'Brian seemed to spend all his time in his laboratory or at home,' she argued in a more reasonable tone. 'He wouldn't have had time for another woman.'

'Are you sure the amount of time he spent at work wasn't a symptom of something wrong at home?' He felt he had touched a nerve and hoped to coax more information from her. 'It often is, you know.'

She considered the suggestion, but shook her head. 'I

41

don't think so. Brian was a very conscientious person. Teaching and doing research are both full-time jobs. Just keeping up with the literature is a major operation. When I was a student there were probably five or six relevant papers each month. Now there might be a hundred.'

Mitchell sensed she was deliberately steering the conversation away from Barry's domestic circumstances, but he wanted her to relax and keep talking. 'Why are there so many papers all of a sudden?'

'The number of scientists has grown exponentially over the last decade and there's tremendous pressure on academics to publish,' she explained. 'Job and promotion prospects all depend on publications.'

She yawned and Mitchell glanced at his watch. It was nearly two o'clock. 'I'm sorry. I hadn't realised it was so late. I'm sure you want to get to bed.'

'Have another drink, if you like. I don't imagine I'll get much sleep tonight anyway.'

He was tempted, but he knew that after another whiskey he'd be ready to stay up all night drinking and tomorrow threatened to be a busy day.

He had a twinge of compunction as he noticed the nearly empty bottle on the sideboard. 'I drank a lot of your whiskey. I must take you out for a drink some time.'

'Don't worry. I was glad of the company.' She seemed reluctant to let him go. 'I'm sorry for talking so much.'

'Don't you mind being here by yourself?'

'I'll be all right. I'm used to being on my own.' She absently stroked a cat that was sitting washing itself on the hall table.

She had to reach past him to open the front door. He found his hands resting on her shoulders and he kissed her briefly on the lips. 'We'll do that. We'll have a drink together some night.'

She disengaged herself without comment and closed the door behind him.

* * *

He must be losing the run of himself, Mitchell thought ruefully as he parked the car near his flat. To hell with it, he decided as he turned off the engine. He'd kissed Catherine Gildea because she was lonely and she was a good-looking woman and it was two o'clock in the morning. He was as lonely himself and he'd spent what was supposed to be his evening off looking at yet another dead body.

Exhaustion caught up with him and he sat staring out into the darkness. The rain had stopped but everything was still sodden, and large drips fell from the trees onto the roof of the car. Maybe he was getting too old for the job, because he had no stomach for this case. He was depressed by the prospect of boring interviews with boring people telling him stupid little lies that would have no connection with Barry's death. He would waste valuable time ferreting out small secrets. At the end of it all he still might have no idea why Brian Barry had died, or, even if he knew, might have no evidence that would stand up in court.

For once he'd forgotten his native caution and shown a bit of feeling for the woman, even though she was an important witness. And, he felt constrained to remind himself as he shook off his inertia and climbed out of the car, if his doubts about Barry's death were shared by the pathologist, Gildea might turn out to be his best suspect in a murder case. He'd better watch his step.

When this was cleared up he would ask her out for a drink. But what would they find to talk about once the case was over? What interests had they in common except Brian Barry's corpse? She'd have no time for the things that interested him, like football and hurling and . . . . He tried to think what his other interests had been before the job had taken over his life. Failing to remember any, he banged the front door and took the stairs two at a time.

The flat seemed more than usually cold and unwelcoming, and he hurriedly undressed and rolled into the unmade bed. Divil mend all women, and academic women in particular, he thought as he tried to make himself comfortable.

Despite the whiskey, sleep didn't come quickly, and he kept more disturbing thoughts at bay by planning the day ahead. He'd have to see O'Loughlin before the superintendent left for the court. He badly needed the forensic evidence before questioning Barry's colleagues. The fingerprints section should have a report for him in the morning and, with luck, Maurice Keane might be able to tell him something by midday. He prayed that the evidence would prove conclusively that Barry had killed himself, but intuitively he knew that it wouldn't.

4

When the alarm rang at seven thirty, Mitchell emerged
from sleep aware of something pleasant just below the
surface of his consciousness. He lay quite still, knowing
the sensation would evaporate if he stirred, until the
scene on Catherine Gildea's doorstep came back to him.
In the sunlight, which was beginning to penetrate the
dusty window, his recriminations of the previous night
seemed absurd.

He studied himself critically in the bathroom mirror
before he started to shave. As a lad he had been secretly
rather vain about his thick, dark curly hair, but now he
had to admit it was more grey than black and, as he
turned his chin towards the window, the stubble was
silver in the morning light. So much for all this genetics
— hadn't his father been as black as a seal when he died
at seventy. He must be taking after his mother, whose
hair had been white as long as he could remember.

All the same, considering he'd had only five hours
sleep, the old face didn't look too bad for forty-three. The
skin under his grey eyes was creased and the lines from
nostrils to chin were deeply etched, but he thought that
these gave him a look of experience. His nose had been

broken in a collapsed scrum so many years ago that he didn't even notice its odd shape any more.

He sang to himself as he finished shaving, but made a face at the mirror when he reached the chorus and discovered that the song he had chosen was 'There's no denying Kitty is remarkably pretty'.

'Devious thing the old subconscious,' he muttered as he wandered into the kitchenette and plugged in the kettle. He cut two slices of bread and slid them under the grill. He thought of phoning Catherine to make sure she was all right but decided she'd probably think he was soft in the head if he did. Thinking about her, he stood gazing at the cooker until the smell of burning reminded him of the toast.

* * *

Superintendent O'Loughlin's office was still empty when Mitchell reached headquarters. In his own room next door he found Sam Smith with a teapot in his hand, waiting for the kettle to boil.

Despite having stayed in the college until the small hours of the morning, Smith looked fresh and rosy-cheeked. His wiry red hair had been combed within an inch of its life and battened down with water but undisciplined curls were already springing free behind each ear.

'Got anything for me yet, Sam?'

'I'll have a cup of tea for you in a minute, sir.' Smith had so much the look of a country lad that, even after five years working together, Mitchell was still sometimes startled by his strong Dublin accent.

'I won't say no to the tea but I'd prefer something more substantial, like a report from the fingerprint boys.'

'If you wanted a report from fingerprints this morning,

46

sir, you should have called them in on Wednesday,' the sergeant said offhandedly as he poured boiling water into the pot.

'Spare me the wit and repartee this morning, Sam,' Mitchell warned. 'Phone the Bureau. Tell them to get off their backsides. I want a report on that gun within an hour.'

Smith shoved a mug of tea into the inspector's fist but it didn't stem the flow of instructions. 'When you've done that, get out to the O'Meara Building as fast as you can. I want the laboratories kept closed until we get the autopsy report. The people who work in the building can go as far as the coffee room in the centre block. I'll probably want statements from all of them today, so keep them there, but don't let anybody, and I mean anybody, into either of the wings. I've got to see the super, and then I want a word with Mrs Barry, but I'll be out to the college as soon as I can.' Mitchell sat down and inspected the messages on his desk 'Will you phone the Press Office too, Sam, before you go out.'

'They've been on twice already this morning, sir,' Sam said plaintively, betraying his almost paranoid dislike of the media. 'The evening papers need a statement before eleven. The Press Office wants to know if we've anything to add to what was released last night.'

'What did we say, Sam? I haven't looked at the papers yet.'

'Just the minimum.' The sergeant picked up the newspaper lying on his desk and turned to the front page. 'We confirmed that we are investigating a fatal shooting incident at the college.' He ran his finger down the column to locate the salient paragraphs. '"A full forensic investigation is in progress and the State Pathologist will carry out a postmortem examination of the remains this morning." And we haven't ruled out foul play.'

47

'Well, we can't add much to that. I suppose we can say,' Mitchell searched for a suitably anodyne phrase, 'that, we're keeping an open mind, pending the outcome of the postmortem.'

While Mitchell drank his tea and made some phone calls, he could hear Sam explain, mostly in words of four letters, the urgency of a preliminary forensic report. As the sergeant truculently slapped down the receiver, Superintendent O'Loughlin stuck his head around the door.

'Good morning, lads. How did you get on in the groves of academe? Sergeant, if there's tea in that pot, you might pour me a cup.'

'Good morning, sir.' Mitchell followed the superintendent into his office. 'I think we have a problem out there: it looks like suicide but smells a bit like murder.' He outlined the circumstances while the elder man filled and lit his pipe.

'As a pipe-smoker yourself, sir, could you imagine, God between us and all harm, blowing your brains out with one hand while you clutched a lighted pipe in the other?'

O'Loughlin chose to regard the question as rhetorical. 'What do you think yourself?' He peered at Mitchell through the haze of smoke that now enveloped him.

'I think it was murder, sir.' Mitchell surprised himself by his own certainty, and qualified it immediately ' — but we'd better watch where we're putting our feet. If we turn the college inside out with a murder enquiry and then there's a suicide verdict at the inquest, we won't be very popular for exposing the family and the university to so much adverse publicity.'

'I can hear the questions in the Dáil now.' The superintendent winced at the prospect and puffed disconsolately at his pipe. 'What about Barry's family?' he eventually asked, obviously hoping that a suspect might be found ouside the world of learning and political influence.

'I talked to the widow last night, sir. I had to break the news to her. She took it well but I think she was genuinely shocked. There's a brother who fancies himself as a militant republican. I've asked the Branch to check up on him. They know him well but say he's harmless; he's just a mouth.'

'Very well, Mitch,' the superintendent nodded his bald head with resignation. 'I suppose you'd better concentrate on Barry's colleagues.'

'Will you be free after the court adjourns this afternoon, sir? We should know more about the case by then.' Despite his impatience with his superior's extreme circumspection, Mitchell respected his judgement.

'He'll probably adjourn early, since it's Friday. I'll be out to the college by five o'clock. You can buy me a drink.'

* * *

The blinds were down in all the windows of the Barrys' house and a formal, black-bordered card pinned to the front door notified callers of the family's bereavement.

Bangharda Brennan answered the door and showed Mitchell into the front room.

'How's Mrs Barry this morning?'

'She's as well as can be expected in the cirumstances, sir.' Brennan's reply was automatic but she added, with genuine concern, 'I don't believe the creature got a wink of sleep last night, but she's a strong woman.'

'Ask her if she feels up to talking to me for a few minutes.'

'I think she'll be glad to see you, sir. She's been asking a lot of questions this morning that I'm not in a position to answer.'

Mitchell could hear women's voices in the background while he looked around the room. It was tastefully but not expensively furnished in neutral shades of beige and umber. A shaft of sunlight sneaking round the edge of a blind fell on a silver-framed photograph of the family. It had been taken in summer, in a garden where Anna Barry and three boys were sitting on the grass. She was looking up at her husband, who, clad only in shorts and sandals, was pushing a small girl in a wheelbarrow. Brian Barry hadn't been a handsome man but the intelligence in the eyes and the muscular vigour of the torso made him the focal point of the picture. He was grinning at the camera but the smile was distorted, Mitchell noted wryly, by the pipe clenched obstinately between his teeth.

'Mrs Barry says will you come and have a cup of coffee?' Maureen Brennan led the way into the kitchen, where Anna Barry and her mother-in-law were sitting at the table.

'Good morning, inspector. I'm glad you've come.' Anna Barry's manner was composed but she looked pale and exhausted. Her blonde hair, which she had worn in an elegant style the night before, looked limp and lustreless, but it was neatly tied back with a black ribbon. The pallor of her face emphasised the fine texture of the skin and her strong bone structure. On a better day, Mitchell realised, she would be a very handsome woman.

'Now that a little of the numbness has worn off, I realise that Brian's death cannot possibly have been an accident.' She looked at Mitchell searchingly as she handed him his coffee. 'I suppose you were trying to tell me that Brian had taken his own life.'

'Honestly, Mrs Barry, we don't know yet how your husband died. He was found in his office with a gun beside his hand.' Mitchell met the level gaze of her dark brown eyes. 'You're right: it's unlikely that the shot could have been accidental. For the moment we are treating the death as suicide, but until we have more evidence we can't be sure.'

'I find it hard to believe that my son could have killed himself,' the elder Mrs Barry said quietly. 'God knows, everybody must say that when it happens to one of their own, but I can't think of any possible reason. For the life of me, I can't even imagine where Brian could have got a gun.'

'Are you sure he had nothing on his mind?'

'I've been thinking of nothing else all night, inspector. Trying to recall if anything unusual had happened recently or if Brian had seemed different in any way.' Distress was making Anna Barry breathless, but she swallowed some coffee and continued in a calmer voice. 'He was a bit preoccupied in the last few months, and he has been very busy.'

'But he didn't seem depressed or out of sorts,' her mother-in-law agreed. 'Mind you, Anna, he could be very secretive, particularly about anything unpleasant.'

'When Brian was worried about something, he tended to bottle it up,' Anna Barry explained. 'It was a protective instinct. He thought he could take the troubles of the world on his shoulders and keep them away from those he loved.'

'You're sure there was nothing that might have been on his mind?' Mitchell was insistent. 'Any problems with the children, financial anxieties, health worries?'

She shook her head. 'His health was generally very good. Financially, we're relatively well off, thank God. We've almost finished repaying the mortgage on the house. Brian had a good salary and I've been able to work a few afternoons a week since Granny came to live here.'

'I suppose the professor had life insurance,' Mitchell suggested.

Anna Barry looked startled. 'I hadn't thought about that — but we had a joint policy. Either of us would get fifty thousand if the other died before sixty.' She seemed slightly cheered by the realisation. 'But there's probably a clause about suicide,' she added vaguely, and immediately lost interest in the subject.

'Had your husband made a will?'

'When we got married we both made wills, leaving everything to each other. I don't believe he made one since. I'd better phone the solicitor and ask him to start looking for the file.' She sighed. 'I suppose I ought to do something about making arrangements for the funeral too.'

'I'm afraid it won't be possible to have the funeral for another few days.' Mitchell hesitated, trying to be tactful. 'Not until the pathologist releases the remains.'

Anna Barry nodded distractedly, overcome by the bureaucracy of death.

'There haven't been any problems with the children, Mrs Barry?' Maureen Brennan prompted her gently.

'They can be a bit of a handful, but they haven't done anything awful recently.' Automatically, she looked over her shoulder through the window into the garden, where two boys were chasing each other tirelessly around the lawn. 'That's what I can't understand. Brian was such a good father. He took his responsibilities to the children very seriously. I can't imagine any motive that could have been strong enough to make him abandon them.'

She looked as if she was about to cry but Mitchell distracted her by asking quietly, 'When did you see your husband last?'

'Yesterday morning.' She glanced at her mother-in-law for confirmation. 'He left here about eight o'clock. He always had lunch in College. He said it was his only opportunity to meet colleagues from other departments.'

'Did you expect him home for tea?'

'No, the Institute centenary function was on last night. I thought he was going to that.'

'You were going out yourself anyway, Mrs Barry, weren't you?'

'Yes, it was a bridge club night.'

'What time did you leave the house?'

She looked a little taken aback by the question, but answered readily enough. 'I went out about seven o'clock. The competition starts at half past seven but my partner didn't turn up, so I didn't play, but I sat in on a few hands and had a drink. That's why I was home earlier than usual, soon after ten o'clock — about half an hour before you and Catherine arrived.'

'Who looked after the children while you were out?'

'Granny was here with them all evening.'

Mitchell stood up. 'I'll be back when I know more about the circumstances of your husband's death.'

* * *

It had been a wet spring and the grass on the football pitches was a penetrating green. It must have been ten years, Mitchell thought, since he'd seen the college by daylight, the time his youngest brother got his veterinary degree. The place had been just an enormous building site, but time and the landscape gardeners had been at work, moulding piles of rubble to grassy banks and blurring the hard edges of concrete with flowering cherry and weeping willow.

There were students everywhere; students with bicycles, with books, with hockey sticks and squash rackets.

Thank God I resisted the temptation. It would have been a soft couple of years, all right, Mitchell conceded, as he slowed down to let a group of young men with hurleys cross the road in front of him. Lectures, coffee, football and pints of porter, but where would I have been at the end of it all with a BA and no job?

A young man in a green anorak, with a tape recorder slung over his shoulder, was hovering outside the O'Meara Building. He recognised Mitchell and pounced on him before he could get out of the car.

'I'm Declan O'Boyle from "News at One",' he said with the breathless intensity he employed for even the most tedious news items. 'Can you tell me if any progress has been made on the Barry shooting?'

Mitchell pushed open the door of the car, deflecting the microphone that was thrust into his face. 'Mr O'Boyle, the Garda Press Office issued a statement earlier this morning,' he said impatiently. 'I have nothing to add until I see the postmortem report.' He turned on his heel and escaped into the building, where an elderly sergeant greeted him with relief.

'Good morning, sergeant, everything under control?'

'It is, but I'm glad you've got here, sir.' The sergeant took off his cap and scratched his head thoughtfully. 'I'd understood that people who work in the university led a very leisured sort of an existence. Maybe this particular collection aren't typical but every bloody one of them, staff and students, has some vitally urgent experiment that makes it absolutely essential that they be admitted to their laboratories immediately.'

'You refused them, I hope, sergeant.'

'I did, sir. I said I was acting on instructions and referred them to my superior officer. There must be about twenty of them who insist on seeing you, the instant you arrive, to explain why an exception has to be made in their particular circumstances.'

'Sergeant, explain to them again, like a good man, that the answer is "no", and get rid of them for me.'

54

'I'll do that, sir, but there are some animals to be fed and watered and a couple of the students say they have machines in the laboratories that might be dangerous if they're not attended to.'

'Very well, sergeant, arrange an escort for whoever feeds the animals. Use your judgement about the others. If you think there's a genuine hazard, let them in, one at a time, under escort, but only for long enough to do whatever is necessary.' The sergeant was about to request further instructions but Mitchell forestalled him. 'Is Sergeant Smith here?'

'No, sir. The university authorities have provided an office for you in the Administration Building. That's the big building across the lake. The sergeant said you'd find him in room 206, sir.'

'Thank you, sergeant. Keep up the good work.'

Like most police officers, Mitchell was used to feeling at home in a variety of environments. However, since setting foot in the college, little more than twelve hours previously, he had persistently felt at a disadvantage, disoriented and not fully in command of the situation. He sensed that he was operating in a society whose customs were arcane, language ambiguous and scale of values different from his own. Now, entering the Administration Building, he found himself in familiar territory again.

With relief, he realised that the administrative offices of all large organisations, be they banks, airlines, universities or even police forces, are universally indistinguishable. The lobby was spacious and its colour scheme predictably bland, except for an abstract canvas that covered most of one wall. The opposite wall was almost obscured by an assortment of exotic plants, the expensive perfection of their foliage identical to their cheaper, plastic counterparts. Apart from a glass box occupied by a uniformed porter, a circular coffee table and some low chairs were the only furnishings.

Asserting his rapidly returning confidence, Mitchell ignored the porter and took the lift to the second floor. He made a mental note to point out to the authorities that security in the building could be improved. The porter was not doing his job properly, allowing a stranger to use the lift.

In room 206 he found Sam, seated behind a vast but empty desk.

'Inspector, you found your way all right? The porter just phoned to tell me you were on your way up.'

Mitchell grinned, recalling the old joke about safaris: for every tiger you see, five tigers see you.

'Dr Keane's just been on, sir. You're to phone him back. He wouldn't tell me a thing.'

Mitchell drummed the desk impatiently while he waited to be put through to the pathologist, but when he finally found Maurice Keane, got little satisfaction. The pathology report would not be available until after the weekend. He was about to slam down the phone when Keane relented. 'I'll tell you this much: none of the medical evidence suggests suicide. All my conclusions are negative, so I won't be able to swear that Barry didn't fire the gun, but, between ourselves, I'm convinced that the man was murdered.'

'What have you found?'

'It's what I haven't found that bothers me: no sign of powder burns around the wound. That's influenced by the individual weapon and by environmental conditions. You'll have to get a second opinion from the ballistics experts, but I'd say that indoors, using a gun of that calibre, the shot must have been fired from a distance of at least two feet — at a conservative estimate. Barry wasn't a big man so that's the limit of arm's reach. In my experience that's not the normal way, if self-destruction

56

can ever be considered a normal act, to put a bullet in the brain. The determined suicide puts the barrel of the gun against the temple or in the mouth.'

'What about the hands?'

'Not a trace of powder on either hand,' Keane said triumphantly, as if clinching the argument. 'That's another thing, Mitch. Did you know your man was left-handed?'

'Can you tell from the autopsy?'

'Not for certain, but there are usually indications. In this case the left hand is slightly bigger than the right and the left arm muscles much more developed.'

'You're probably right. Barry used his left hand for most things — which makes me sceptical about the notion that he shot himself with the right hand.'

'I think somebody is trying to mislead us, Mitch.' Keane chuckled delightedly. 'Well, I can never resist a challenge. I'll do every test in the book to prove this wasn't suicide.'

'Can you confirm the time of death, Maurice?'

'No mystery there. My report will state that death occurred between eight and nine o'clock and that the bullet wound appears to be the cause of death. Otherwise, Barry seems to have been very fit.'

'Then we can eliminate serious illness as a possible motive for suicide?'

'Yes, he's a very healthy corpse.' Keane gave another macabre chuckle.

Mitchell grimaced. He liked to think of himself as a hard man, but he could never get used to Keane's ghoulish intimacy with death. He thanked him perfunctorily and put down the receiver. Before he had taken his hand from the phone, it rang again.

Sergeant Thompson of the Technical Bureau was also less than forthcoming. 'There's no question of a final report until early next week, sir. Friday is always busy and we're very short-staffed, but I can tell you, unofficially of course, what we've got so far. The gun is a Webley .45. We don't see many of them these days. They were standard issue to British officers during the war. There used to be a lot of them around. They turned up fairly frequently in IRA weapon caches — the homes of ex-officers were regular targets for break-ins when guns were in short supply —but your modern terrorist wouldn't be bothered with that sort of obsolete rubbish. Of course,' he insisted righteously, 'the bullet hasn't been sent over from Pathology yet, so we can't prove this gun fired the fatal shot.'

'Any fingerprints on it, sergeant?' Mitchell wasn't going to be side-tracked into internecine wrangling.

'One nice clean set of the deceased's prints, a textbook set, you could call them — nothing else. Too neat for suicide,' Thompson said with uncharacteristic lack of equivocation.

'Are you saying that the gun was wiped clean of prints? Before or after it was fired?'

'This will all be in the report, sir, when we've had time to do further tests.' The sergeant was obviously regretting his candour. 'But preliminary examination suggests that the gun was thoroughly wiped, then handled with gloves and the deceased's prints imposed on it after it was fired.'

'Will you be able to prove it?'

Thompson was immediately cautious. 'It'll be chancy. It mightn't survive a good defence counsel.'

'Get those tests done right away, sergeant. If you're right, this is a murder case, so give it priority.' Before the sergeant could embark on a protest, Mitchell continued relentlessly: 'I need a fingerprint team back out here immediately. I want every door and window tested for prints and I want prints taken from everybody who works here.'

Thompson launched into a detailed explanation of the impossibility of this request, but Mitchell cut him short. 'I know it's a tall order, sergeant, but it's an order.'

Mitchell banged down the phone and relayed the information from both calls to Sam Smith. 'It looks as if we have a murder enquiry on our hands.' He felt distinctly more cheerful now that his doubts had been resolved. 'We'd better start asking some questions. I want every person who works in that building interviewed, just for starters.'

'That's quite a job, sir,' Smith replied with ill-concealed relish. 'I got a list from the people here: there are nine teaching staff, ten technicians, and a secretary. There are also about twenty postgraduate students doing full-time research, and a dozen undergraduates doing projects in the laboratories.'

'I'll talk to the academic staff.' Mitchell stood up as if eager for immediate action. 'Organise a team to interview the technical people and the students, especially the three who were in the building last night. Maureen Brennan will be out here after lunch, so get her to help you.' He stood at the window, looking across the lake at the O'Meara Building. 'We'll keep up the pretence of suicide but I want to know where everybody was between eight and nine o'clock last night and I want their fingerprints. Find out how well each one knew Brian Barry. Ask about Barry's movements yesterday and get the details of any disagreements or arguments he may have had recently.'

'I'll get interview rooms organised in the O'Meara Building.' Smith was in his element. 'And arrange the fingerprinting.'

'Stress that it's only for elimination, Sam. I don't want any student protests about police harassment.'

5

Robert Roche looked vigorous for his sixty-two years. A big man, his bulk suggested muscle rather than fat and, although his white hair was thinning on the crown, skilful barbering had created an illusion of plenty. He was dressed in a three-piece suit of dark brown tweed flecked with heather colours, a cream silk shirt and an ancient club tie.

Mitchell looked speculatively at the tie and jotted a query in his notebook. He wondered how Roche would react to being interviewed from the wrong side of his own desk, but the professor gave no sign of finding the situation incongruous. He selected a comfortable-looking chair from several standing against the opposite wall and placed it close to the desk, so that he was seated directly facing the inspector. Obviously well versed in dealing with the world under a variety of conditions, Roche's voice and facial expression were expertly controlled. The smile with which he greeted Mitchell was warm, but his demeanour acknowledged the seriousness of the occasion.

'I appreciate what a difficult situation this must be for you and for the department, professor.' Mitchell felt called on to exchange civilities before getting down to business.

'A tragedy, inspector.' Roche rested his elbows on the arms of the chair, made a steeple of his fingers, and looked over them at Mitchell. 'Had Brian's death been from natural causes, or indeed an accident, it would be tragic enough, but under these circumstances it's shattering.'

'Professor Barry was a close friend?'

'I can appreciate, inspector, that your enquiry into the reason for Brian's death obliges you to establish his personal relations with other members of the department.' Roche eyed Mitchell thoughtfully for several seconds before saying crisply, 'I'll be frank with you. You would eventually hear what I'm going to tell you on the departmental grapevine. In fact I shouldn't be surprised if you had heard already?'

Mitchell ignored the note of interrogation, and Roche continued, 'Fifteen years ago the chair of genetics, which I now hold, became vacant following the retirement of old Professor O'Meara. Both Conor Dodd and I were candidates. Brian strongly supported Conor.' He paused and, taking a pair of black-rimmed spectacles from his breast-pocket, put them on and studied the inspector for some seconds. 'I hope nobody in the department would say that I have been vindictive as a result. We have all tried to forget the past, but inevitably there was a coolness between Brian and myself.' He paused again. 'I don't want to make too much of this, but it's better that you hear it from me than as a sinister rumour.'

Roche signalled the end of his recital by sitting back in his chair and taking a cigar case and a gold lighter from the pocket of his jacket. Mitchell shook his head at the proffered cigar. He felt slightly disconcerted that Roche should light up without as much as a by-your-leave, until he remembered that they were, after all, sitting in the other man's office.

He waited for the ritual of cigar lighting to be completed before nudging the interview forward. Tilting his chair back, he looked squarely at Roche. 'Usually, nobody wishes to speak ill of the dead, and the information we get is often bland and consists, at best, of half truths, so I appreciate your frankness.' A cloud of fragrant cigar smoke wafted across the desk. Automatically, Mitchell took his pipe from his pocket, but a vision of Barry's fingers clutched claw-like around his pipe flashed through his mind, and he laid it unfilled on the desk. 'In the absence of a suicide note, the coroner will expect us to furnish evidence of Professor Barry's recent state of mind. Did you see him yesterday?'

Roche drew on his cigar and thought for a moment. 'I had a few words with him at coffee yesterday morning. The last time I talked to him at any length was probably Thursday of last week. We played squash and had a drink together afterwards.'

In response to Mitchell's look of surprise, he explained, 'For the last six months or so Brian and I played squash every Thursday evening. He had recently taken it up and wanted an opponent who was not too formidable. I used to play quite a decent game, but I can't move as fast as I could forty years ago. Brian was a natural sportsman with a good eye for the ball and the additional advantage of playing left-handed, so we were fairly evenly matched. It was a convenient arrangement and I believe both of us welcomed the opportunity to attempt a rapprochement. We usually took a drink together afterwards.' Roche peered over his glasses at the inspector as if to assess his reaction. 'We still had very divergent opinions on many things, but we were learning to respect each other's views.'

62

Mitchell nodded. 'What can you tell me about Barry's state of mind. Was he depressed?'

'He always was a bit of a worrier. He took his responsibilities to his students very seriously.' Detecting a note of wonder in Roche's voice, Mitchell suppressed a smile as he thought of Catherine Gildea's judgement on the professor.

'But last Thursday,' Roche, unaware of his interlocutor's amusement, continued, 'he seemed to have some problem on his mind. I wouldn't say he was depressed — perhaps preoccupied would be a better word. Mind you, I don't believe I would have remarked on it except for what has happened.'

'You didn't have your usual game of squash yesterday?'

'No, inspector, we were both going to the centenary function of the Science Institute — at least I assumed that Brian would be going. It's sad to think that if yesterday had been a normal Thursday, we'd have been playing squash at half past eight.' He sighed theatrically. 'Perhaps Brian would have been able to sweat out whatever was on his mind, instead of doing what he did.'

'You attended the Institute function yourself, sir?' Mitchell was determined to bring Roche's attention back to the point.

'I'm president of the Institute this year. I had the honour of chairing the lecture.'

'I'm puzzled about the nature of the celebration. Was it a party or a serious academic occasion?'

'I can certainly understand your confusion, inspector.' Roche agreed readily. 'It was a mixture of both and, personally, I don't mind telling you,' he leaned forward in his chair, 'that neither of them was an unqualified success. The council was divided into two opposing schools of thought on the most appropriate way of celebrating the centenary. Some people felt that a serious meeting with

63

scientific papers was called for; others, including myself, believed that a dinner would be more celebratory. Eventually we compromised and agreed on a dinner preceded by a formal lecture by this year's medallist, who happened to be my colleague Conor Dodd. To allow an opportunity to circulate and chat to old friends, we had a sherry reception between the lecture and the dinner.'

'Could you give me a rough idea of the timetable?'

Mitchell thought Roche was about to object, but he evidently thought better of it. 'We started the lecture punctually at seven o'clock. Conor spoke for no more than an hour, and I kept my contributions as short as possible, so it was probably about ten past eight when we started the sherry. I think the dinner began soon after nine; coffee had just been served when Catherine phoned me with the news about Brian. That was a little after half past ten.'

'All the staff were invited to the function?' Mitchell made no effort to disguise the drift of his questioning. 'How many of them were there?'

'Actually I had thought everybody would be there, particularly as Conor was giving the lecture — everybody except David Morgan, that is. I made a point of inviting David, but he excused himself on the grounds that he had so much work to do. To tell you the truth,' Roche lowered his voice, 'I think he's finding life here a bit tough. He's newly married and his wife hasn't found a job, so things are probably a bit tight financially.' He shook his head in sympathy with his young colleague, but added impishly, 'He doesn't take a drink, so he may also find our social functions a bit too alcoholic for his taste.'

'Which of your colleagues attended the function?' Mitchell was becoming impatient of the professor's digressions.

'Let me see. Conor was there, of course.' Roche drew deliberately on his cigar, unmoved by Mitchell's irritation. 'I was talking to young Paul and Colette during the sherry reception. I didn't see Chris O'Mahony, but I'm sure he must have been there. There really was quite a large crowd.' Roche smiled appeasingly. 'Well over a hundred sat down to dinner, so it wasn't possible to see everyone.'

'You expected Professor Barry and Dr Gildea to be there?' Mitchell led him, grateful that there was no defence counsel to protest. 'Have you any idea why they didn't go?'

'No, inspector. I was surprised that neither of them was there. Brian was a member of council and both he and Catherine were regular attenders at the meetings. Catherine told me this morning that, unexpectedly, she had to stay back to look after a student and, presumably,' Roche gazed at the light fitting over his head, 'poor Brian had other things on his mind.'

'This rule about staying late with students — is it strictly adhered to?'

'Not always, I'm afraid. I think some staff are less conscientious about it than they should be.' Roche pursed his lips in disapproval. 'It really is quite important; our insurers insist on it.'

'So if students want to work late, lecturers have no choice but to stay on?'

'They have the option of packing the student off home,' Roche said emphatically, 'but some staff are reluctant to do that if it means ruining an experiment, so the student gets a lecture about starting earlier in the morning and the lecturer misses supper.'

Roche stubbed out his cigar with an air of finality. The gesture would normally have provoked Mitchell to prolong the proceedings, but realising that he still had six of

Roche's colleagues to see before five o'clock, he brought the interview to a close.

* * *

As Conor Dodd entered the room, Mitchell wondered idly if height was a selective advantage for geneticists. Dodd was at least two inches taller than Roche, but probably carried three stone less. However, despite his advantage in weight and years, he seemed neither as fit nor as vital as the older man.

'I'm sorry to have kept you waiting.'

Dodd sat down, his long limbs untidily disposed, in the chair that Roche had just vacated, and peered myopically at Mitchell through gold-rimmed glasses. 'In comparison with the tragic loss this department has suffered, any inconvenience is minor. I can't quite believe what has happened. Have you any idea what the reason was?'

'Not yet but I hope that you or one of your colleagues may be able to provide an explanation.'

'Brian was a very old friend as well as a valued colleague. I will do everything I can to help.' Dodd leaned forward towards the desk as if to convince Mitchell of his co-operation.

Instinctively, Mitchell tilted his chair back. 'Do you know of any worries on Barry's mind or anything unusual in his behaviour?'

Dodd removed his spectacles and cleaned them pensively on the end of his tie. 'I am as bewildered as the rest of my colleagues. I would have described Brian as a contented man. He was somewhat introverted and his attitude to his work and his family was extremely conscientious.' Dodd replaced his glasses and examined Mitchell carefully, as if focusing on him for the first time. 'Those characteristics, inspector, if taken to extremes, suggest a personality that might ultimately suffer a breakdown, but in Brian they were balanced by a sense of humour and, if I'm not sounding too pretentious, by spiritual values that gave him a sense of proportion.' Dodd cleared his throat self-importantly. 'With regard to his recent behaviour — being wise after the event — I noticed that he was under some sort of pressure. He seemed more tense than usual, but at the time I simply put it down to the end of a long term, when, as you can imagine, inspector, we all get a little overwrought.' Dodd sat back complacently as if he felt he had made a major contribution to Mitchell's knowledge.

'When did you last talk to Barry?'

'I had a short conversation with him in his room yesterday morning,' Dodd answered without hesitation. 'That was the last time I saw him. I wasn't here yesterday afternoon. As you probably know, I was giving a rather important lecture last night and I needed to put some last-minute thought into my text, so I worked at home after lunch. I find one is less liable to interruption there than in one's office.'

'What did you talk about?'

'It was a purely routine matter about practical classes.'

'You noticed nothing unusual about Barry?'

'No,' Dodd said categorically, but then seemed to reconsider: 'except perhaps that he seemed less relaxed than usual. I was probably on edge myself, so we kept the conversation to essentials.'

'Did Barry refer to your lecture?'

'Oh, no,' Dodd insisted impatiently. 'We only discussed routine, administrative matters.'

'I'm trying to establish why Barry didn't attend your lecture. He made no reference to his intentions when he spoke to you?'

'Now that I come to think of it, inspector, as I was leaving his office Brian made a gracious comment about looking forward to hearing my paper.' Dodd smiled boyishly. 'I can't recall his exact words but I got the impression that he intended to be there. Catherine Gildea says he had to stay back with a student, but I suppose the reality was that he wanted some place to be alone to . . . .' Apparently finding it unpalatable to complete the sentence, he finished lamely, 'Really, inspector, I find it quite impossible to contemplate.'

* * *

Catherine Gildea had referred to Chris O'Mahony as an extrovert, and, from the moment he entered the room, Mitchell could see that the description was apt. His blond hair curled in an unruly mop, initially almost obscuring his eyes. As he sat down opposite Mitchell, he brushed the hair back from his forehead with an impatient gesture, revealing eyes of a penetrating blue. He seemed ill-at-ease, in striking contrast to the assured manner of both his senior colleagues. Mitchell guessed that he was suffering the embarrassment of the perpetual joker, totally at a loss when confronted with a situation demanding a serious response.

Answering routine questions seemed to restore O'Mahony's confidence, and he relaxed a little. However, after some discussion it became clear that, like his colleagues before him, O'Mahony was unable to supply a credible reason for Barry's death.

'Inspector, are you absolutely convinced it was suicide?'

'As you may have seen in the newspapers,' Mitchell was surprised by the question, but replied blandly, 'our statement was noncommittal. However, we are satisfied that the shot could not have been accidental.'

'I didn't suppose it could have been.' O'Mahony was dismissive. 'Isn't there the possibility of murder?'

'Why do you suggest that?'

'Brian wasn't the suicidal type,' O'Mahony said dogmatically. 'He was far too serious.'

Before Mitchell had a chance to argue with this proposition, O'Mahony insisted, 'I know that people think it's the quiet, serious types who can become sufficiently depressed to end it all. But it's not. It's the manic types — like me.'

O'Mahony seemed taken aback by his own candour but hurried to justify his assertion. 'We're really much more likely to be unable to cope when things go wrong and to take the so-called easy way out. A serious, responsible person like Brian would feel it was his duty to see things through.'

'I take your point.' Mitchell was genuinely struck by the young man's argument. 'Actually, we haven't ruled out what we quaintly call foul play. That's why we're asking so many questions. For instance, when did you last speak to Barry?'

O'Mahony hesitated before saying, 'I'm sure I've seen him around the building several times in the last few days, but I probably haven't spoken to him for a while.'

'Any particular reason?'

'I'm afraid Brian rather disapproved of me. He thought I was irresponsible. He's been quite cool with me since I played a rather silly joke at a party last Christmas. I owed everybody an apology, but I wasn't going to eat crow. Now, of course, I'm sorry. I actually liked the guy.'

'Then you won't mind telling me where you were last evening?'

'Oh, I have an alibi, inspector. As a loyal colleague, I attended Conor Dodd's lecture and the dinner afterwards.'

Mitchell didn't argue the point.

* * *

By five o'clock, Mitchell had interviewed the other four

69

available lecturers. Paul Mooney, who struck Mitchell as being the least imaginative of the academics, said he talked to Brian Barry regularly, as their laboratories were on the same corridor. He seemed to accept unquestioningly that Barry had killed himself, although insisting that there had been nothing strange about him recently. He himself had been in the Burlington Hotel from half past six the previous evening until nearly midnight and had been in the company of his colleague Dr Lalor virtually all evening.

Colette Lalor confirmed that she had been with Mooney throughout the centenary function. She was bright and blonde, and her warm, humorous personality showed through her distress at Barry's death. Mitchell resisted the temptation to query her sanity for spending so much of her time with the unworthy Mooney. She could give him no help with his enquiries about Barry. Although she had greatly liked and admired him, she rarely saw him, except at staff meetings. Their offices were in different wings of the building, and, since she herself had little time for anything other than fruit flies, they had few common scientific interests.

David Morgan seemed even more shy than on the night before, so Mitchell cut his losses and dismissed him, after taking a brief statement about his movements on the previous evening.

His last interview of the afternoon was with Catherine Gildea, but that was also perfunctory. Although she was open and friendly with him, she had little to add to what she had already told him.

6

Superintendent O'Loughlin was already waiting when Mitchell got back to the Administration Building. Sam Smith had done wonders since the morning and had transformed the office into something resembling an incident room. He had acquired another desk and a large electric typewriter, on which Maureen Brennan was already typing a report. Files, stationery, directories and the other paraphernalia of police paperwork were stacked on the shelves; two large maps, one of the campus and the other a city street map, were tacked to the wall.

Mitchell was happy to see that the sergeant had also succeeded in requisitioning an electric kettle, a large teapot and some mugs decorated with the college insignia. Smith stood up and plugged in the kettle as soon he saw the inspector.

'How is the court case going, sir?' Mitchell threw his briefcase onto a desk and greeted the superintendent.

O'Loughlin looked up reluctantly from the sports results. 'Slowly, very slowly.' He folded the *Evening Press* methodically and slipped it into the pocket of his jacket. 'With McSweeney as defence counsel, every shred of evidence will be examined with a fine-tooth comb. The buggers will probably get off on a technicality at the end of the day, but McSweeney won't look for that until he has a couple of weeks' fees under his belt.' He shook his head pessimistically. 'It could go on for another fortnight. You'll be long finished here by then.'

'I hope so, sir.' Mitchell shifted a pile of box-files from the only unoccupied chair. 'But don't count on it. This looks more like murder than suicide.'

O'Loughlin took his pipe from his pocket and started to clean it out with his penknife. 'How many murder cases have you worked on, Mitch?'

'Probably twenty, sir, not counting a few menial tasks while I was still in uniform.'

'What a violent society this has become!' the superintendent commented wistfully. 'I must have been twenty years in the force before I worked on my first murder enquiry. It was the talk of the country for months then. We knew who had done it, but none of the neighbours would tell us a thing, and our forensic methods weren't up to much in those days, so it never came to court.' He sighed nostalgically as he knocked his pipe out vigorously into a large china ashtray. 'What have the experts to say about the case in hand?'

'I've made some notes on the preliminary forensic evidence.' Mitchell took two closely written pages from his briefcase and handed them to the superintendent. 'None of it is consistent with suicide.'

O'Loughlin absently held out his mug. 'I could do with another drop of tea, sergeant.' Smith refilled the mug and the superindentent sipped tea while he perused the notes.

Mitchell lit a cigarette and gratefully accepted a mug of tea from Sam. He turned his chair slightly so that he didn't have to watch the superintendent. He wanted him to agree that this was murder and would argue passionately against any alternative view but if a verdict of suicide were to prevail he could go home now, take a night off, and forget about recalcitrant academics.

O'Loughlin returned the notes to Mitchell without comment. He looked around at the three officers and said quietly, 'All right, lads. This is a murder enquiry.'

Brennan stopped typing and opened her notebook at a clean page. Smith plugged in the kettle again. Mitchell, his ambivalence forgotten, felt a surge of adrenalin and wanted action. He jumped up and paced restlessly to and fro in the confined space between the two desks. 'According to my interviews this afternoon, Brian Barry had no enemies, was admired by his colleagues and respected by his students,' he declaimed as he strode towards the window. 'Nevertheless,' he turned on his heel and paced slowly back towards them, 'the man was shot dead in a locked building to which only his colleagues and students have keys.'

'And where were they all between eight and nine o'clock last night?' O'Loughlin had got his pipe going nicely and was willing to humour the inspector.

'Of the nine academic staff, one is away in Canada and one is now dead.' Mitchell had come to rest with his back to the window, both elbows leaning on the sill. 'I interviewed the remaining seven this afternoon. Five of them claim, conveniently, to have been in the same place: at a function in the Burlington Hotel. They should be able to provide alibis for each other, and so presumably should the other hundred odd guests at the function. The other two academics were in the O'Meara Building at the time of the shooting but they were at opposite ends of the building, and neither saw the other until after the event.

'There are ten other staff: nine technicians and a secretary. Did you manage to see them all this afternoon, Maureen?'

'I did, sir, and they can all account for their movements. The secretary was having dinner with her fiancé. All the technicians claim that they left the building around five thirty and they have alibis of one sort or another,' she paused to consult her notebook, 'ranging from night classes to drinking in their local pubs or being at home with their families.'

'They'll all have to be checked,' Mitchell and O'Loughlin said in unison. The two younger officers looked pained by this statement of the obvious.

'What about the postgraduate students? Have they been interviewed?' Mitchell asked. 'They frequently have to be in the building after six o'clock when the doors are locked by the security staff,' he explained to the superintendent, 'so each of them has a key.'

'We have statements from all but two of them.' Smith picked up a file and flicked through the pages. 'Owen O'Neill, the only postgraduate who was here when Barry was killed, stayed back to help his girlfriend, Maeve Carty, who is an undergraduate. He says he was with her in the basement when the shot was fired.

'The rest insist that on any other evening they'd have been in the labs but they took last night off because one of them got married yesterday. They all went to a party at the bride's home in Dun Laoghaire, so they claim they can provide alibis for each other. Those who hadn't already reached the party by eight thirty were on the way there in a group. At the time of the shooting,' he referred to the file, 'they'd got as far as the Carraig in Blackrock. The two we haven't seen are the bride herself, who is adequately vouched for by her guests, and a young lady called Whelan who, by all accounts, was the life and soul of the party — so much so that she is still sleeping off her hangover and won't be available for interview until tomorrow.'

'I suppose you wouldn't find undergraduates around at that hour of the night?' O'Loughlin was jotting down a list of queries on the back of an envelope.

'They're allowed on the premises if a staff member is there, sir.' Smith picked up another file. 'There were two in the building when Barry was shot. Maeve Carty confirms that she was with the boyfriend, young O'Neill, all the time. I also had a word with Peter McCormack, the other undergraduate who was on the premises. Barry was his supervisor, and in fact the ostensible reason for Barry's presence here last evening, was to keep an eye on him. However, McCormack says that Barry was in his office all evening, and he didn't see him after seven o'clock. At the time of the shooting, McCormack claims he was using a piece of equipment in the other wing of the building.'

'Isn't it a bit too convenient that so many suspects chose to congregate in groups at a safe distance from the scene of crime?' O'Loughlin looked at each of the three in turn.

'Look at it the other way, sir,' Mitchell abandoned the window-sill and came back to sit opposite the superintendent, 'and it suggests that our murderer knew that it would be a nice quiet night in the laboratories so that he could come and go without being noticed.'

'It's too neat and tidy.' O'Loughlin was sceptical. 'If we eliminate the two in the basement, only three people appear to have had the opportunity to shoot Barry. Could one of them have a motive?'

Mitchell said nothing. This was the question he didn't want to think about.

'There was no love lost between young McCormack and his supervisor, sir,' Smith volunteered. 'He implied that Barry had treated him unfairly about his project and was making him do a lot of extra work.'

75

'We'd better talk to that young man again,' Mitchell said quickly, welcoming the diversion.

O'Loughlin wasn't easily diverted.'What about the two academics?'

'David Morgan is a relatively new member of staff,' Mitchell explained. 'He's an earnest young man who concentrates on his work. He's unlikely to harbour any hostility towards Barry.' Unconsciously, Mitchell rooted through his pockets and took out his cigarettes. Finding the packet in his hand, he placed it unopened on the desk. 'Catherine Gildea, on the other hand,' he spoke slowly and deliberately, 'has been on the staff for thirteen years and was Barry's postgraduate student before that. They were friends and scientific collaborators. She found the body and certainly had the opportunity to fire the shot herself, but there's no evidence of motive.'

'Might she and the professor have been more than good friends?' O'Loughlin suggested.

'As far as I know there was nothing of that sort going on.' Mitchell brushed the insinuation aside rather too quickly.

O'Loughlin looked at Mitchell over the tops of his glasses. Without turning round, he said over his shoulder, 'Sergeant, I'm sure you and Miss Brennan must have a lot to do. There's no need to keep you from whatever you should be doing.'

Smith took the hint immediately, picked up his notebook and took Brennan's jacket from the back of the door. 'Come on Maur, you'd better have a word with the cleaning supervisor and I've got to make sure those lads from the Technical Bureau know what they're supposed to be doing.'

As Smith closed the door, Mitchell got up and started leafing through the papers on the desk. O'Loughlin watched him. 'Did you question this woman?' he asked eventually. 'What's she called — Gildea?'

'At length.'

'Did you ask her about her personal relations with the deceased?'

'I did not.' Mitchell felt his temper rise, but aware that he was over-reacting, he sat down and grinned disarmingly at O'Loughlin. 'I'm not that blunt. I had a long chat with her last night after we broke the news to Mrs Barry. She was quite open with me about feelings between staff within the department, but I got no hint of an emotional relationship between herself and Barry. Besides,' he added righteously, 'Mrs Barry and herself are obviously very close, which would hardly be the case if there was anything improper in her relationship with the professor.'

'In some ways you're a simple soul, Mitch. Catherine Gildea wouldn't be the first woman to be sleeping discreetly with her best friend's husband.'

'I'll make further enquiries about Dr Gildea's relationship with Barry.' Mitchell wanted an end to this discussion. He stood up and started packing files into his briefcase.

'Have you taken a bit of a fancy to the lassie?' O'Loughlin's pipe had gone out and he sat there, striking match after match, vainly trying to relight it. 'I wish you'd marry some nice girl, Mitch, and settle down. You might learn something about women and become less susceptible to their wiles.'

Mitchell was in no mood for banter. 'I hope I know how to keep my personal feelings out of an enquiry by now, superintendent.'

'Come off your high horse, Mitch.' The superintendent, realising he had pursued the joke far enough, was conciliatory. 'I was only pulling your leg, but if the cap fits . . .' He gave up his efforts with the pipe and knocked it out into the ashtray. 'I suppose I'll have to buy you a drink now. Is there anywhere in this godforsaken place that a Christian can get a pint of stout?'

'We can go to the student bar, sir.' Mitchell was annoyed with himself for letting O'Loughlin get a rise out of him, but he wasn't going to turn down the offer of a drink.

The bar was still relatively quiet; most lectures and practical classes wouldn't finish until six o'clock. A few groups of students were scattered around the tables or were playing snooker at the far end of the room. While the superintendent was ordering drinks, Mitchell examined his surroundings. The architect had evidently intended the bar to provide a stimulating environment for young minds. The walls were stark, unfinished brick but the furnishings were in crisp primary colours. The idea was probably successful when the building was new. Now the walls were defaced with grubby remnants of sticky tape where a thousand posters had been torn from the brick, and here and there great thoughts had been inscribed with felt-tipped pens. The carpet had fared no better. Mitchell estimated that several pounds of chewing gum could be scraped from its pile. 'Students are a scruffy lot, sir,' he remarked as O'Loughlin returned to the table carrying two creamy pints of Guinness.

'You're getting old and conservative.' O'Loughlin sat down and looked around. On the wall beside him, 'Support the Gardai — Beat yourself up!' was inscribed in bright green ink. He turned his back deliberately to the legend and picked up his pint. 'I've a son and a daughter who are students here. They don't look any different from these youngsters, but they and their friends are nice kids. They've a sense of responsibility for themselves and for what they call "Planet Earth" that I don't think you or I had when we were their age.'

78

Reluctant to get involved in another argument with O'Loughlin, Mitchell tried to steer the conversation into neutral waters by asking politely, 'What are they studying, sir?'

'One is a final-year engineering student and the other is in first arts.'

'That must be costing you a small fortune. Do you really think it's worth the expense?' Mitchell couldn't resist the question. 'The job prospects can't be too bright, particularly for the girl doing arts.'

O'Loughlin threw back his head and laughed; the inspector had fallen neatly into the trap. 'Oh, Maura will be all right. She seems to be heading for a First in chemical engineering. The young lad is doing classics, so he'll probably end up as the most scholarly man in the dole queue. He's a very bright boy: he got twenty-eight points in his Leaving Cert.' O'Loughlin, beaming with paternal pride, paused for a throatful of stout. Mitchell tried to look impressed, but judged it wiser not to interrupt.

'Yes, young Donal could have gone into medicine or any faculty he wanted,' O'Loughlin continued. 'Everybody tried to persuade him to take a professional degree but the only thing he had any interest in was Greek and I'm proud of him for standing his ground.'

Mitchell was touched by O'Loughlin's obvious pride in his son. It was an unexpected departure from the man's normally cynical outlook on life. But he felt lost for a suitable rejoinder and the two men drank in silence until the superintendent banged his empty glass on the table, waking Mitchell from reveries of his own youth.

'Now, Mitch, there are some points about this case I want to get clear in my mind, but I have an appointment at seven o'clock, so if you're buying I'll just have a small one for the road.'

When Mitchell returned with the drinks, O'Loughlin

reflectively poured a small quantity of water into his whiskey. 'Are we sure that the O'Meara building was locked last night?'

'We're not certain,' Mitchell admitted. 'One of the security men locked the door as usual at six o'clock, but the students would have been in and out after that.'

'It could have been left open accidentally?'

'It could have been left on the latch. However, there was a fierce row a few months ago about the door being left unlocked and the students have been careful about it since then. Gildea had tea with her two students and they came back about half past seven. The door was locked then, and all three remember that Gildea made sure to lock it after them because there was some chat about security in the building. As far as we know, those three were the last people to enter the building before Barry was shot.'

'Are there other doors to the building?'

'There are six emergency exits, four leading onto fire escapes and two on the ground floor, but they're permanently locked with the keys in little glass boxes beside them. They were all in order when we checked the building last night.'

'Cleaners?'

'They don't start until ten o'clock.'

'An intruder, then?'

'There was no sign of a break-in.' Mitchell paused for a mouthful of stout. 'Somebody could have entered the building before six o'clock and hidden in an empty classroom or laboratory. But if he did so with the objective of killing Barry, I can't understand why he didn't do it before eight thirty.'

'Could it have been a casual villain who came across Barry by accident?'

'The attempt to make the shooting look like suicide

suggests not, sir.'

'Could Barry have let his murderer into the building?' O'Loughlin seemed enthusiastic about the idea. 'He could have gone out and brought somebody back with him, or maybe he waited in the hall for his murderer to come, by appointment, to the front door. Why did he absent himself from the festivities at the Burlington unless he had other business to attend to?'

Mitchell shook his head. 'There's nothing in his diary, except a note about the Institute centenary.'

'You'd better make enquiries whether anybody was seen entering or leaving the building, though I suppose it would have been hard for the murderer to slip out unnoticed once others in the building were alerted by the shot.'

'Gildea is the only one who admits she heard the shot. She took the lift to the basement to make sure her students were all right. I've retraced that route and, at any reasonable pace, at least four minutes would have elapsed between hearing the shot and getting to the first floor, where she found the body. That would have allowed ample time for the murderer to run down the stairs and out the front door.'

O'Loughlin swirled the remains of his whiskey slowly around in his glass. 'We seem to be back to the people with keys. You'll have to start looking for holes in some of those convenient alibis.' He stood up and finished his whiskey in a single gulp. 'Otherwise, you're going to have to ask your friend Catherine Gildea some searching questions.'

Mitchell watched the superintendent as he left the bar, picking his steps fastidiously between rucksacks and other impedimenta strewn across the aisles. The place had filled up while they were talking and all the tables were now occupied by groups of students, cheerful at the end of a week's classes. He tried unsuccessfully to reconcile himself to the notion that any of these youths might be the offspring of the circumspect O'Loughlin in his pin-stripe suit and well-brushed crombie overcoat.

The *craic* was really getting going now. The jukebox had been turned up and heavy metal throbbed from the loudspeakers. A pall of smoke was forming over the room. Mitchell sniffed and thought he caught an elusive sweet tang mixed with the smell of cigarettes. This definitely wasn't his sort of pub. He would be much happier in the company of the Friday-night clientele in Lynch's, but it had been a long afternoon and he needed another pint before he ventured out in the rain.

He moved to the end of the bar farthest from the jukebox. It was much quieter here and the crowd was not as dense. He leaned his elbow on the counter and watched his pint settle. Absorbed by the perennially miraculous transformation of the tawny liquid into black body and creamy head, he suddenly became aware of snatches of conversation from a table behind him.

'Of course if it was Noddy that was shot we'd all know who had killed him,' a girl's voice asserted authoritatively. In response to a feeble protest from one of her companions, she continued, 'Owen, don't be so dim. Everybody knows that Dodd and Roche have been mortal enemies since Roche became professor.'

Every group has one member who knows everything, Mitchell reflected with amusement. Turning round, he identified the speaker as a plump young woman wearing long pendant earrings, which bobbed up and down as she hectored her audience.

'Jacky, you're always unfair to poor Noddy.' Mitchell recognised the respondent as Owen O'Neill and focussed his attention more closely on the group.

'Well, he's so boring,' the one called Jacky insisted,

'going on all the time as if he's an unappreciated genius.'

Another of her companions had the temerity to take issue with her. 'Well, I don't care what you say, Jacky. He's brilliant. You'll find his name in all the textbooks and everybody knows about the Dodd Effect.'

'No they don't,' another student contradicted him immediately. 'The Morgue says he never heard of it before he came to Dublin.'

'Neither had Gerry and he only came from Cork,' Jacky chimed in again. 'It's only because Noddy goes on about it all the time that we think it's important. Anyway, everybody knows now that his theories are all wrong.'

'That's rubbish, Jacky,' another student retorted. 'The papers Conor published last year are really neat, and they prove all his predictions.' He sounded genuinely excited. 'Anyway, the Institute would hardly have awarded him their highest honour if his theories were all wrong.'

Jacky was not prepared to surrender. 'Katy says they awarded him the medal for the work he did years ago.' She spoke slowly, as if trying to make something clear to a rather dull child. 'The old fellows on the council of the Institute are so conservative that it takes them twenty years to make up their minds whether any piece of work is really sound. Katy says Dodd's theories are a load of cobblers.'

The students seemed to have exhausted the subject of their supervisors, and the conversation drifted to the more compelling topic of Ireland's prospects at Lansdowne Road on the following day. Mitchell, anxious to nudge the conversation back into a more informative direction, picked up his pint and strolled over to their table. As he approached, he heard Jacky pontificate, 'Everybody knows that Paul Deane is a better outside-half than Jonathan Davies.'

83

To Mitchell's relief, several of the students recognised him and he was saved the embarrassment of introducing himself. They greeted him with irreverent comments such as, 'Over here looking for clues?' and 'Can you solve the mystery of how they manage to serve such a bad pint here?'

'I hope you weren't subjected to any police brutality today.' Mitchell was glad to join in the banter. 'To compensate, can I offer to buy you all a drink, if you're not too busy?'

Jacky, predictably, appointed herself spokeswoman for the group. 'Actually, we're here at this unusually early hour because you people won't let us into our labs,' she explained righteously. 'You're driving us to drink.'

'Jacky Whelan! You've only just got out of bed,' somebody protested.

'You could go to the library,' another was quick to point out.

This suggestion didn't seem to appeal much to anybody, and Mitchell had no difficulty in persuading them to let him buy a round.

When they had all got their drinks and the *Slaintes* had been politely exchanged, Mitchell steered the conversation back to Professor Barry. 'I believe he was brilliant.'

Several of the students, including the irrepressible Jacky, said that Barry had been their supervisor and agreed that he had been very bright. However, when asked what would happen to their own careers, they seemed at a loss. Only Jacky, who, Mitchell now realised, was a couple of years older than the others, appeared to have given the problem any thought.

'They'll have to appoint somebody new, but that will take for ever. In the meantime poor old Katy will probably have to take us on as well as her own lot.'

'"Katy" would be Dr Gildea?' Mitchell conjectured. 'She and Professor Barry did a lot of work together?'

One of the young men was enthusiastically describing the number of papers published jointly by Barry and Gildea, when Jacky intervened, 'That's not all they did together'.

'Don't be so bitchy, Jacky,' another young woman intervened swiftly, trying to silence her.

However, the interruption only provoked Jacky to elaborate, 'Everybody knows about it. They didn't make any secret of it. They always used to leave together in the evenings and were always in the staff bar together. I've seen him driving her into college in the morning,' she concluded, as if that finally clinched the matter.

'Jacky, you're an incurable romantic,' Owen O'Neill protested. 'Barry used to pick her up from the garage when she left her car to be serviced.'

The indiscretion of having such a conversation in front of the inspector apparently escaped the students because another young man, who had been silent up to this, now chimed in. 'I've seen Barry leave her house in the small hours of the morning.'

'Aidan, you're lying!' Jacky sounded outraged. Mitchell felt she was upset by the prospect of a major piece of gossip of which she was ignorant, rather than by any moral scruples.

'No, honestly, Jacky,' Aidan protested. 'My aunt and uncle live just up the road from Katy. One night I was leaving there very late and I saw Brian get into his car outside her door. My cousin says that his car was often parked there.'

'I can't imagine Barry having a wild love affair,' asserted one of the young women, rather wistfully. 'He was ancient. He must have been at least forty.'

'He was forty-four,' Jacky confirmed, determined to

reassert her authority as the well-informed member of the group.

'How do you know?' the younger girl asked, her faith in Jacky's omniscience clearly shaken by earlier revelations.

'He always keeps his passport in his desk ——'

'— and you always go through his desk when you're there on your own in the evenings,' Owen finished the sentence for her.

'Oh, come on, everybody does that,' Jacky was defensive. 'The staff know we do it. That's why they usually keep some of the drawers locked.'

Mitchell was sufficiently intrigued by this admission to abandon his role of silent listener. 'Isn't it a breach of trust?'

'Honestly, no, inspector,' Jacky sounded quite hurt. 'I wouldn't read anything that was confidential — unless, of course, it affected us. For instance, Barry had a file on this year's fourth years, and I've never peeked at it even once.' She shook her head earnestly at Mitchell, her earrings almost dipping into her pint of stout, but honesty apparently compelled her to add, 'Of course, I did look through his old files to see what he said about me when I was in fourth year. Actually it was rather sweet. He said I had a lot of potential but didn't work as hard as I should. And that's certainly true.'

Nobody rushed to contradict her. 'Anyway, I haven't been able to get near Brian's desk for ages,' she protested. 'He's been locking his office every evening now since Christmas. I don't know what he had tucked away in there, but the place was like Fort Knox.'

'Maybe he was afraid somebody would come in and shoot him.'

Jacky looked witheringly at the author of this piece of bad taste, but turned to Mitchell and asked seriously,

'Inspector, is it true that it wasn't really suicide, that somebody must have killed the prof?'

Mitchell ruefully remembered Catherine's claim that the postgraduates kept themselves well informed. 'Jacky, we're not really sure what happened.'

'Did somebody break in and shoot him?'

'There's no evidence of that,' Mitchell admitted.

'That means the murderer was one of the staff?' Jacky's earrings were dancing with excitement.

'Or a student,' Mitchell reminded her as he stood up and prepared to take his leave. 'You all have keys.'

This silenced all of them except Jacky. 'Can we help you hunt for the murderer?' she asked eagerly.

'Thanks, Jacky, you've been a great help to me already.'

7

As Mitchell drove out of the college, he could feel the effects of too many pints on an empty stomach. He'd had more to drink than he'd intended, but not enough to induce any feeling of well-being, just enough to make him irritable and uncertain of what to do next. He ought to go home and eat, but the Guinness had taken the edge off his appetite. He wanted another drink. It was only half eight. To go to Lynch's now would be a disaster. He'd still be there at two in the morning with a skinful of drink to sleep off.

He got as far as the canal bridge without coming to any decision. Almost without conscious thought, he pulled into the right-hand lane. If Catherine Gildea was at home, he might get some straight answers to the question of her relationship with Brian Barry. The glib way she had spoken the night before of her close collaboration with the professor amused her. Even this afternoon, her formal statement had included the phrase 'close relationship' at least twice and he hadn't picked it up.

As he pulled into a parking space opposite her house, it occurred to him that it might be wiser to wait until tomorrow before confronting her, but the compulsion to discover the truth was stronger than his native caution. He silenced his misgivings by slamming the door of the car.

'Good evening, Dr Gildea. Forgive me for disturbing you at this hour, but there are a few little questions that I think you could help me with.' Mitchell enunciated each syllable with the exaggerated clarity of the not-quite-sober.

Catherine Gildea was obviously not expecting company. She was wearing a loose sweater over a pair of faded denim jeans, and her head was swathed in a large white towel, which gave her a withdrawn, nun-like air.

She showed no surprise at seeing him on her doorstep, and smiled as she shooed the cats out of the way to let him into the hall. 'Come in and have a drink, inspector.'

'No, thank you, Dr Gildea. I'm still on duty.'

She raised her eyebrows a fraction and he realised that, in the close confines of the hall, she would be able to smell the Guinness on his breath.

He felt an idiot and wished that he had gone straight home. 'You were having an affair with Barry?' His sense of inadequacy made him blurt the question out in an attempt to regain his authority.

She picked up a cat and stroked its head. 'What makes you think so?' She looked up at him without expression, but he felt she was laughing to herself.

'I'll ask the questions, if you don't mind, Dr Gildea. I'd be obliged if you'd give me a straight answer.'

She stood there holding the cat, and her self-possession provoked him to add spitefully, 'I took your advice and spent half an hour talking to your postgraduates. They were very helpful.'

'Is this off the record?'

'Nothing is off the record in a murder enquiry.'

'In that case, the simple answer is: "No, inspector, I

was not having an affair with Brian Barry. We were just good friends." If that is all you wanted to know, then please don't let me waste any more of your valuable time. I'll show you out.' She made as if to move towards the front door.

'Look.' Mitchell stepped forward so that he stood between her and the door. 'I can do this the hard way and take you down to Irishtown, where you can make a formal statement.'

'It would be no trouble for me to "accompany you to the station" and to "help you with your enquiries", but you'll find out nothing that way. If you'd stop behaving like a Redemptorist preaching hellfire and damnation and be prevailed on to sit down and have a drink, I'll try to tell you the truth about my relationship with Brian.' She deposited the cat on the hall table. It stalked down the polished surface towards Mitchell and rubbed its head against his sleeve.

'But it will be off the record,' she added quickly. 'I can't put this in a signed statement. I don't see that any of it's relevant to your enquiry.' She turned defiantly towards the stairs. 'Come down to the study. It will be warmer, I've a fire lighting there.'

Mitchell desperately wanted to sustain his bad temper towards her, but he had absently started to tickle the cat's ears. It was impossible to retain a tone of authority in the circumstances. He also badly wanted a pee, and a drink. He gave in and meekly followed her downstairs.

She took his anorak and showed him where to find the bathroom. It wasn't a particularly feminine bathroom, but there were no signs of a male presence. There was a razor socket beside the washbasin, but no razor on the shelves or in the cabinet, and there was only a single toothbrush in a blue china mug beside the basin.

She looked questioningly at him when he came into

the study. She probably thought he'd invented a need to use the bathroom as an excuse for having a look around. Well, that was his job, whether she liked it or not.

A cat was curled up in one of the armchairs beside the fire. She ejected it, shook out the cushions and offered the chair to Mitchell.

'I thought you had only two cats.'

'Just the two. I know it seems more, they move around a lot.'

He relaxed and looked around the room. It was very different from the "good" room she had entertained him in last night. This was where she lived and worked. The room probably doubled as study and dining room. A large table, pushed back against one wall, was covered with heaps of notes and books and a word-processor. Books and papers were also scattered on the floor around the other armchair.

'I was trying to do a bit of work, but my mind wasn't really on it.' She gathered up the papers from the floor and dumped them on the table. 'To be honest, I'm glad of an excuse to pack it in and have a drink.'

She didn't ask him what he'd like to drink, but he could hear a reassuring clink of bottles as she rooted in a cupboard behind his chair.

'You said "murder enquiry". You're finally convinced Brian didn't kill himself?' She handed Mitchell a large whiskey.

'I've even managed to convince the superintendent.'

She had poured herself an equally large whiskey, and set it down on a small table beside the other armchair. 'And he suspects that I was Brian's mistress and that I killed him.' She was adding water to the whiskey but her hand shook and the water spilled on the table.

'Were you?'

'Yes, I was.' She swabbed the spill neatly with a tissue.

The displaced cat had by now taken possession of her armchair, but she scooped it up and sat down with it in her lap. It purred loudly and dug its claws joyfully in and out of the fabric of her jeans. She ignored the animal but looked over its head at Mitchell, expecting a response. He was silent. Now that she had said it so bluntly he felt a cold shock in the pit of his stomach. He really didn't want to hear any more about it, but she would insist on telling him everything now.

'I once had a love affair with Brian, but that was ages ago, and for years we have been nothing more than close friends.' She sipped her drink, apparently in no hurry to continue. 'The irony,' she said eventually, 'is that none of the postgraduates could have known about the affair. Even Jacky, who no doubt was one of your informants, has been in the lab for only five years and my relationship with Brian was over long before that.'

She lit a cigarette and inhaled the smoke deeply. 'When I was a student I was really terrified of Brian. He was awfully kind but he seemed so brilliant. I was amazed to discover that he thought I was one of the brightest postgraduates in the department.'

'Did he tell you that?'

'No, but I happened to see a reference that he wrote for me.'

Mitchell couldn't help a grin. 'You mean that, even in your time, postgraduates went through their supervisor's desk?'

'You must have grilled our poor students if you forced them to admit that.'

'Oh, don't worry. They were quite forthcoming about it. They seem to regard it almost as a duty of their station in life.'

She laughed. 'They subscribe to John Philpot Curran's theory that the condition of liberty is the fruit of eternal vigilance! They have a point,' she admitted. 'In my case, reading that reference bolstered my self-esteem and helped me survive the American academic jungle. It also changed my perception of Brian.' Another long pause followed. Mitchell resisted the impulse to question her: let her tell the story at her own pace. She talked a little of her time in America, her return to Dublin after three years. 'I was delighted when Brian suggested collaborating on some research. We got on well together and had an essential ingredient in our first project: luck. Fortuitously, we hit on the right approach to the right problem and so were able to publish half-a-dozen papers within two years.'

She stroked the cat absently while she gathered her thoughts. Mitchell sensed that she was approaching the difficult part of her story.

'You understand that Brian had been married for several years at this time,' she said quickly. 'Anna and Brian were very hospitable, and I became almost one of the family. About two years after I came back to Dublin, Brian and I were invited to read a paper at a scientific conference in Holland. It was in the early summer. We flew to Amsterdam on a Sunday. We spent the evening walking by the canals, talking about our work. There were tulips everywhere, the trees were just coming into leaf and Brian and I were discussing the structure of the bacterial chromosome.' She spoke fluently now, with an almost hypnotic rhythm. Listening to her, Mitchell relaxed, his eyes focused on a vivid abstract canvas over the fireplace. He couldn't decide whether it was supposed to be a scarlet bird entangled in a yellow net or a woman with a basket on her head.

'I remember that very clearly. I remember thinking that anybody watching us strolling together would think we were lovers. We stopped for dinner at an Indonesian

93

restaurant. By the time we left there it was almost dark and the lights from all those tall narrow houses were reflected on the water. There was a barrel organ playing somewhere. The warm swampy smell that the canals give off at night —' she thought about it for a moment. 'I suppose it's a mixture of hydrogen sulphide and methane,' she decided prosaically — 'they should bottle it because it must be an aphrodisiac. Suddenly we weren't talking about genetics. We weren't talking about anything.'

Mitchell stopped staring at the painting and looked at her sharply, but she seemed hardly aware of his presence.

'I realise now that if it hadn't happened in Amsterdam it would have happened at some other time. I don't believe that two young adults can spend eight hours a day in each other's company without becoming, at least, sexually curious about each other.' She paused again, but this time with the air of somebody who has accomplished the most difficult part of a task and looks forward to completing it. 'We had a wonderful week. We were both carried away with the sheer fun of being in love. Brian wasn't by any means the first man in my life, but this was quite different from anything that had gone before.' She took a large mouthful of whiskey, and said quietly, 'We knew it couldn't last. We thought it would be possible to return to our former platonic friendship.'

Restlessly, she pushed the cat off her knee and stood up. 'You know, it's a great relief to tell you all this.' She picked up the whiskey bottle and replenished both drinks. 'You're the only person that I can tell. I can't grieve for Brian properly as a valued colleague and a scientific collaborator. He was once my lover. Part of me wants to do something daft, make a big dramatic gesture of grief, like throwing a single rose into his grave.'

Mitchell watched her without comment. He realised she was probably rather drunk.

'But I won't, because of Anna.' Pulling the cushion from the armchair, she sat down on the floor in front of the fire. She unwrapped the towel from her head and pushed her damp hair back from her face. 'That's how it all began,' she said matter-of-factly. 'But you're probably more interested in how it ended.'

Mitchell nodded and watched her run her fingers through her hair. It was as if he had never looked at her before. In the firelight, the contours of her face had softened. Animation, and whiskey, had heightened her colour, so that her skin glowed. She glanced up and caught him studying her, and he wondered how he could have thought her eyes were hard.

'We thought we could go on as if nothing had happened.' She laughed at the memory. 'We tried to avoid each other, but everything conspired against us; we met at every turn. At first the relationship was fraught. We both felt guilty at deceiving Anna, but', she shrugged philo-sophically, 'you rationalise situations, and we learned to live with it.'

'Weren't you ever afraid of being found out?' Mitchell, despite himself, was caught up in the story.

'We were very discreet. I don't believe anybody realised that we were more than friends.' She shook her head impatiently, anxious to conclude. 'Our relationship con-tinued for nearly four years, until Brian decided that he needed time away from teaching, or from me, and accepted an offer from Harvard to spend a year doing research there. We wrote to each other, of course, but our letters were mainly taken up with technicalities.'

She held her glass towards the light and contemplated the colour of the spirit. 'I met another man. I realised how pleasant it was to be able to go out to dinner or the theatre with him.' She grinned, aware that she was straying from the point. 'Brian stayed in Harvard for eighteen months. I was looking forward to having him back in the lab but knew we couldn't resume our relationship. He agreed without argument, probably because he too wanted to end the affair. Anyway, he wouldn't have tried to persuade me to continue a relationship against my will.'

Mitchell was looking perplexed. 'Wasn't it awkward for both of you after the affair broke up — being thrown together so much, having to see each other every day at work?'

'Not at all.' She seemed quite surprised by the question. 'In fact, things worked out quite well. I was still awfully fond of Brian, of course, and enjoyed having him to talk to again. I had slipped into bad habits while he was away, not really concentrating on research. But once he was back, I settled down and we published some important papers over the next couple of years. Ironically, because we now had nothing to hide, we started to spend time together quite openly. We frequently worked late and went for a drink together afterwards, in a pub or to Brian's house, or here. Hence the students' unshakable conviction that we were having an affair. In fact, Anna often joined us, but the students couldn't know that.'

Mitchell felt that some comment was called for, but the warmth of the fire and the effect of the whiskey on top of several pints were lulling him into inertia. He was also conscious of his own sexual arousal in response to Catherine's account of her love affair. He knew he should get up and leave, but before he could pull himself together she said suddenly, 'You shook me when you asked last night if there could be another woman in Brian's life. I wondered had you guessed about me, but, more to the point, I had suspected recently that there might be somebody else.'

'What put that idea in your head?' Mitchell was immediately wide awake.

'In the last few months Brian seemed to have changed. He became quite . . . ' She searched for the right adjective. 'The only word is "shifty". He avoided being alone with me. We never went for a drink together — he always seemed to have some excuse.'

'How long had this been happening?'

'It's hard to put my finger exactly on when it started but I think it was after the Christmas vacation. In recent years Brian and I had established a routine. On Mondays and Thursdays, Anna played bridge; on Thursdays, Brian played squash; on Mondays, we usually both worked late and then went for a drink. At the beginning of this term, when we went out together, Brian was very quiet, almost sullen. I tried to make conversation but all I could get were monosyllabic replies.' Her voice was less calm now, it had become sharp with anxiety. 'When I asked him what was wrong, he was defensive. He apologised for being bad company and said he was a bit preoccupied but it was nothing that I need worry about.'

'What made you think he was seeing another woman?' Mitchell put the question quietly, reluctant to disturb her train of thought.

'At first I couldn't think what was wrong. I wasn't aware of any problems in the lab. It wasn't a family problem because I phoned Anna and she seemed in particularly good form. It finally dawned on me that it *had* to be another woman; there just didn't seem to be any other explanation. Brian had been in Germany before Christmas, and I decided he must have met somebody there — history repeating itself, in a way.

'Of course I was very jealous and hypocritical. I went around asking myself, "How could he do this to Anna?" Eventually I became reconciled to the situation, but then even my working relationship with Brian started to deteriorate.

'For twelve years,' she begged him to understand, 'Brian and I discussed every detail of our research with each other. Suddenly, in the last two months, when I asked him about some projects, he became evasive.' She reached out and took a cigarette from the packet on the table. 'I spent most of the Christmas vacation drafting a paper on some work we'd done together. The manuscript has been on his desk since January. Each time I tried to discuss it with him, he put me off with excuses about being busy.'

She was trying to light her cigarette but her lighter wouldn't work. Mitchell stood up and lit it for her. 'Everybody I talked to this afternoon said he had been preoccupied recently.'

'I hate to think that Brian had something on his mind that he felt he couldn't talk to me about.'

He placed his empty glass on the mantelpiece. 'Barry may have felt, with some justification, that it was safer for you to know nothing about his problems.' He glanced at his watch. 'It's time I went home.'

She jumped up as if recharged by the luxury of confession, and started tidying the table, sorting notes into neat piles and pushing everything to one end. 'I'm sure you haven't had supper. Why don't I make an omelette for both of us. I was just about to make one for myself when you arrived.' She took a folded cloth from the cupboard and spread it deftly over one end of the table. 'After so much emotional disclosure, I'm absolutely starving.'

'It's very kind of you to offer, but under the circumstances, I couldn't accept.'

She ignored his refusal and started taking cutlery out of a drawer. He felt he had better elaborate. 'The situation is a bit awkward.' He stirred the turf in the fire with the toe of his shoe. 'You were in the building at the time of Brian Barry's death. There's no evidence of motive, but your close relationship with Barry raises questions.' He gave a nervous laugh. 'I don't want to eat your salt tonight and find I have to charge you with murder tomorrow.'

She put down the pile of plates she was holding, taken aback by his bluntness. Then she laughed. 'How typical of the Irish male! You've been happily drinking my whiskey all evening but you're getting qualms of conscience because I offer you an egg!'

She stopped laughing abruptly and came to stand beside him at the fireplace. 'You can't think I killed Brian after what I've told you? I loved Brian. His death is going to leave a vacuum in my life that I'll probably never fill.'

'For God's sake, I'm not accusing you of anything.' Acutely embarrassed, he turned his head away and muttered, so that she could scarcely hear, 'Love and hate are strong emotions, and the line between the two isn't always clear.' He threw himself back into the armchair. 'All right, Catherine. Cook me an egg.'

8

'Well, this is a bit more than the simple egg you offered me,' Mitchell protested as Catherine Gildea placed omelettes, a salad and a cake of brown bread on the table.

'Don't just sit there.' She handed him a bottle of wine and a corkscrew. It was a Muscadet-sur-lie. He liked a drop of wine with his dinner. He hadn't tried this sort before, he usually preferred red, but the Lord knew what it would do to him on top of the pints and the whiskey.

As he poured the wine, she suggested, 'Let's forget your enquiries for a while and talk about something else. I've bored you all evening with the story of my life, now it's your turn. Tell me about yourself.'

'There's not much to tell.' He knew that sounded boorish but he wasn't used to talking about himself. 'I told you I'm from Kerry.' He paused, wondering what else might interest her. 'My father was the local school-master — that was back in the good old days of the one-teacher school. It's closed now and the kids go by bus to Killorglin.'

She seemed interested enough but she didn't say anything more, and they ate in silence, both hungry after a long day. He paused to sip his wine, and said suddenly,

'When I was thirteen I got a scholarship to boarding school. My parents were fierce proud of me, but I didn't like it all that much. I didn't feel that I fitted in with the boys there. Oh, I was popular enough. I was good at football — rugby, of course — but I'd played Gaelic as a kid, and if you're good at one you can usually make out all right at the others.' Having got over his initial reticence, he was positively garrulous now. 'But I found that most of the boys were from a different background to mine, city lads, sons of doctors and barristers. They were friendly enough, but I always felt the odd man out. Then I found I was also the odd man out at home in the holidays. The local lads thought I was stuck up because I went to a posh school and played rugby. Of course, all I wanted was to play Gaelic again, but they wouldn't let me play in any of the league matches because of the ban on "foreign games".'

'You must have been very clever to win a scholarship.'

'I was bright enough,' he admitted without pretension. 'I had learned to do my work, being the master's child.' He put his knife and fork down and leaned back in his chair. 'My father was very much the old-fashioned schoolmaster, interested in local customs and folklore and he was a bit of a classical scholar too in his way. He taught me Latin and Greek while I was still at national school, so the book-learning was never a problem for me.'

He spread butter carefully on a slice of bread. It was a long time since he had talked so much about himself. 'The parents were terrible disappointed when I joined the Guards. The mother had visions of me joining the Benedictines, and my dad wanted me to go to university to study classics or at least to do something useful like medicine or law. I suppose it must seem strange to you,' he looked up to see how she would react, 'but I hated the thought of going to the university. It wasn't that I didn't want to study — that never came hard to me — but I wanted to be with my own people, ordinary country lads with no side to them. I thought coming up here to the university would be just like school again.'

He wanted to provoke her to a defence of academic values, but she refused to rise to the bait.

'Why did you become a policeman?' She asked the question with an air of polite interest but he felt she was challenging him to justify his existence.

This was something he usually avoided thinking about. He gave her his standard reply: 'It was just coincidence: the job came up at the right time.' She wasn't willing to accept it, and allowed a silence to develop between them that forced him to elaborate. 'I always admired our local sergeant. He knew everything about the parish, not just the people but every plant and animal within miles, and, of course, every fish.' He paused to gauge her reaction. She seemed interested, and he felt on safer ground. 'Himself and the old man used to go fishing for salmon together on Sundays — poaching, needless to say, not a licence between the pair of them. Of course, they were dead safe. The water bailiff and the sergeant used to drink together after hours in the local pub, so no fear there'd ever be any trouble.'

'So the sergeant was what our sociologists would call your "role model"?'

'Yes,' he agreed enthusiastically, missing her irony. 'I used to think he had a great life.'

'And that's what you wanted for yourself?' She made no attempt to disguise her lack of conviction.

'I'll tell you what happened. Just before I did the Leaving Cert, there was this advertisement in the paper for Garda recruits. One night at school a few of us sent in applications, for a joke really. When the Leaving Cert results came out, it turned out I had done well enough to get a scholarship. At home, everyone kept telling me to do this subject, or there'd be more money in that one, or a better job from the other, until I was sick of the whole performance. When the call to Templemore arrived, it seemed providential. I told them all to keep their scholarships and degrees, and went off to become a garda.'

'You were never sorry?'

'Not really.' He felt the need to counter her scepticism. 'I sometimes regret disappointing my parents,' he conceded. 'My father had a real love for books and learning, and I think to the day he died he never entirely forgave me. But the poor man never said a hard word to me about it.' He drifted into a long silence, playing with the crumbs on his plate.

'Never mind your parents. Are you happy?'

'It's hard to know.' Mitchell admitted. He felt less defensive. 'I loved my time at Templemore. It's very strict, but after boarding school I didn't find it too bad, and sure I knew how to get around the rules. I was able to play Gaelic football again and I became a bit of a star on the depot team. The exams weren't much of a problem either.'

'But you're not so happy now that you're a fully fledged policeman?' she hazarded.

'My first few years in uniform were great. I was posted to the wilds of Mayo and I had a powerful time there. The local crime statistics were how many drunks we rounded up on market day. The rest of the time was fishing and football and plenty of young lassies down from Dublin on their summer holidays.' He decided he'd better not dwell on that aspect of his past and changed tack. 'The old sergeant there was great. He took a bit of a liking to me because I was good at the paperwork, which wasn't his strong point at all. He used to be always on at me to do the exams for promotion, but I knew when I was well off and kept telling him I'd do them next year, but he must have stopped believing me after a while because the next thing I knew I was posted to Dublin on traffic duty.' He laughed and put his hand confidingly on Catherine's wrist. 'The old bastard admitted years afterwards that he'd fixed it up with the deputy commissioner. They'd been in the War of Independence together.'

'I thought you said he liked you.'

'Oh, he had my good at heart, I have to admit that. I'd grown too fond of the life of a country gentleman, so he had me shifted to a rotten job where the only way out would be to get the exams. He was right on both counts. I hated the job, and I got first place in the exams within six months. And I've been stuck in Dublin ever since.'

'It's not that bad!'

'Sorry, I forgot you were a Dub. I suppose it's all right,' he conceded grudgingly, 'but I miss the outdoor life and the job is getting more and more sordid all the time. A lot of it is just sifting through endless piles of paper, and that way it's not so different from any civil service job, but every so often you realise how much violence and human suffering you're dealing with and it gets you down.'

As if to assuage his frustration, he drank off the wine in his glass. 'The irony is that if I'd done as my parents wished and studied law, I could have ended up where I wanted to be. The last time I was down home, the first person I met in the pub was a lad called Dick Houlihan, who was in my class at school. He was from a very posh family and I always thought he had big ambitions. Dick became a solicitor. He spent a couple of years as a junior partner in a Dublin firm, then his father died and left him a few quid. The money bought him an office in Killorglin and a house in Glenbeigh. Now Dick employs two bright young graduates to run the practice for him, and was able to take me fishing every afternoon I was home.'

The wine bottle was empty. Mitchell looked at his watch. 'Now, Catherine, it's high time I was leaving. You have me talking far too much. I've surely got my own back on you.'

He stood up from the table and put his hand lightly on her shoulder. 'I'm sorry I was bad-tempered when I came here tonight. I thought you had a lot of questions to answer but here we are, at the end of the night, and it's myself doing all the talking. It's your own fault. You shouldn't have given me so much drink.'

She stood up and studied him critically. 'Let me make some coffee before you go. I don't suppose the local guards would have the nerve to breathalyse you, but there's no point in taking chances.'

All his professional instincts told him to leave now, right away, but he heard himself saying, 'I'll let you make coffee if you let me wash the dishes.'

He was aware of an overwhelming feeling of irresponsibility, as if, having missed the opportunity to leave, the situation was now entirely outside his control. He moved slowly, stacking the plates carefully and brushing the crumbs off the table. He carried the dishes to the kitchen and placed them neatly in the sink before coming to stand just behind Catherine who was spooning coffee into a percolator on the cooker. He knew she was aware of his nearness, but she didn't turn to face him until he spoke her name. Even then, she replaced the lid of the coffee tin carefully and put the top on the percolator before turning slowly into his arms. He kissed her gently. She seemed to share his inertia, because when he finally released her she said nothing but remained close to him, resting her head on his tweed jacket.

He buried his nose in her hair. It was dry now but she hadn't combed it out and it hung in a loose tangle on her shoulders. 'You must be a changeling — your hair smells of the sea.'

She drew back from him and he could see that she was laughing.

'Don't laugh,' he insisted, 'I'm trying to be romantic.'

'I'm sorry.' She giggled. 'If you'd ever smelt the sea in Dublin Bay, I hope you wouldn't say that about my hair.'

'That's not the sea! I'm talking about the Atlantic Ocean, and it smells of wind and salt and sun.'

'Don't be absurd, Mitch. There's no sun in the west of Ireland!'

He let her go and turned and looked out of the large window into the back garden. Four pale yellow eyes regarded him balefully from the darkness.

'You ought to put bars on that window,' he warned her, inconsequentially, 'or you'll be having unwelcome visitors some night, and I don't mean Watson and Crick — or me!'

'You're never unwelcome,' she insisted, 'even tonight when you turned up ranting about fornication like a drunken parish priest.'

He sat down at the kitchen table and lit cigarettes for both of them. 'I don't know what to say. I wish to God we'd met under other circumstances — at a dance or in a pub. Things would be more natural between us, and maybe you'd take me seriously.'

She was still standing in front of the cooker, adjusting the flame under the coffee-pot until the water percolated at the right speed, emitting a rhythmic thunk. 'I'm taking you too damn seriously. I find it just a bit intimidating that, only an hour ago, you were warning me that you might have to charge me with murder!'

'I know I must seem a complete fool. There I was having scruples about letting you give me supper. No wonder you're laughing at me!'

She sat down opposite him and took the lighted cigarette he held out to her. 'I wasn't laughing at you. Things are happening too fast for me, and I'm a bit hysterical.' She drew deeply on her cigarette and exhaled slowly, watching him through the smoke. 'I think I could care about you, care about you very much, but I'm not in any state of mind to know.' She squashed out the cigarette decisively. 'However, I'm willing to take a chance on it.'

* * *

Mitchell woke to the smell of cigarette smoke. Catherine was lying on her back, her profile just visible in the early dawn light.

'Aren't you afraid of burning the house down if you fall asleep with a cigarette in your hand?'

'I'm wide awake.'

'How do you feel?'

'A bit guilty,' she admitted.

'I'm sorry. I'm a self-centred bastard, amn't I?'

'It's all right. I only feel guilty in a superficial, "what would people say" sort of way.'

She got up to make coffee and toast and brought them back to the bedroom.

'Can I ask you something?' he said indistinctly through a mouthful of toast and marmalade.

'Michael Mitchell, you've spent most of the last thirty-six hours asking me questions and now you need my permission?'

'What happened to the other man?'

'What other man?' she sounded puzzled.

'The one you said you were involved with after Brian Barry.'

She laughed. 'That was years ago. He folded his tent and slipped away soon after Brian came back from America.'

'You're a fine-looking woman. I just wondered why you had never married.'

'Sexist pig!' she said affably. 'I'm not married because I don't need to be married. I earn a good salary; I own a house and a car. I get more than enough male companionship at work, and I can afford to pay a man to cut the grass and put out the garbage.'

'There's a bit more to marriage, surely, than getting a mortgage and mowing the lawn.' Mitchell was shocked at any woman taking this attitude.

'If I get lonely, I can call a policeman!'

'All right, Katy. I know it's none of my business.'

'I haven't got time to be lonely,' she protested. 'There's always so much work to do: reports to write, papers to read, grant applications to make. I never seem to have any spare time. Of course I have a social life, too,' she added hastily. 'There are lots of parties, and I often go out to dinner, to Brian and Anna, but sometimes to other friends.'

He looked sideways at her, but before he could comment she asked sweetly, 'Now tell me why a handsome, irresistible man like you is still single?'

He shrugged. 'I suppose, like yourself, Katy, I've let myself get too caught up in the job.'

'Mitch, why on earth have you taken to addressing me as "Katy"?' She seemed glad of an excuse to change the subject.

'Don't you like it? "Katy" seems to suit you. I suppose I picked it up from the students.'

'Is that what they call me?' She sounded amazed.

'Didn't you know?'

'God, no. It's something I prefer not to dwell on. I thought it would be a lot worse.'

'They're not very inventive, but consider yourself lucky. Two of your colleagues are known as "Noddy" and "the Morgue".'

She laughed out loud. 'Poor David! It's horribly appropriate; he is rather uncheerful—but who's "Noddy"?'

'Conor Dodd, renowned, I am reliably informed, for the "Dodd Effect". Whatever that might be.'

She giggled. 'Brian used to say it was Murphy's Law of Microbial Behaviour: "Cells under carefully controlled laboratory conditions behave as they bloody well please." Where on earth did you hear about it? I bet Conor managed to mention it when you interviewed him yesterday — he's terribly proud of it.'

'No, the students were talking about it in the bar, but they said it was wrong.'

'Sometimes I despair,' she groaned. 'Those youngsters are graduates, yet they can't distinguish fact from gossip.' She got up from the bed and went to sit at the dressing-table. 'The Dodd Effect is a fact just as Conor first described it back in the sixties. It was by no means an original observation. Every microbiologist since Pasteur has known that the more you feed bugs, the faster they'll grow. However, Conor was the first person to attempt to explain why this is so.' She picked up a brush and aggressively attacked her tousled hair.

'Tell me about it. If you can make it intelligible to someone with Leaving Cert biology.'

She swung around on the stool, turning to face him, her hairbrush arrested in mid-air. 'It's really quite simple — all the best theories are simple. Conor found that two things control the growth rate of bacteria. One is environmental — in other words, the amount of food available — the other is genetic. He studied the relationship between the two and published an elegant series of papers that show how they interact. That's why his name became associated with the phenomenon. Conor's theories were based on sound experimental evidence, but some of his

109

predictions went a little farther than the facts justified. There's always a temptation when you have a good idea to try to apply it universally. I considered that some of his predictions about DNA synthesis and cell replication were incorrect.' She turned back to the mirror and resumed the attack on her hair.

'So you *do* think Dodd's theories are wrong,' Mitchell insisted argumentatively. He was seeing a different side of her personality as she talked about her subject. At another level, he wanted her to turn round again so that he could watch her breasts.

'No I don't.' She turned to face him but continued brushing her hair. 'Conor recently published a series of very good papers that show how the same factors control all sorts of things in the cell, including synthesis of RNA and DNA, and proving most of his predictions.'

She pointed her hairbrush accusingly at Mitchell. 'I bet it was Jacky you were talking to. I can hear her: "Everybody knows the Dodd Effect is wrong."' She giggled at her own impersonation of Jacky but added bitterly, 'I suppose it was "Everybody knows those two were having an affair" too!'

'Don't be cross with me about that. Listening to gossip is part of my job, and you can understand now why I took the news so personally.'

'All right, Mitch.' She had finished brushing her hair and was twisting it into a coil. 'I realise this situation is even less easy for you than for me, but it might help if we both saw the funny side of things, even in this tragic mess.'

He picked up his watch from the bedside table. 'Talking of the job, I'd better go. My sergeant won't see the funny side if I keep him waiting.'

'It's Saturday. Do you have to work today?' she mumbled through a mouthful of hairpins, as he was pulling on his shirt.

'I'm afraid there's no five-day week for coppers.' He stood looking over Catherine's shoulder, trying to see enough mirror to knot his tie. 'I've to meet the super for a meal after the match but I'll be free later. Perhaps we could go for a drink?'

She took the hairpins out of her mouth and looked at him in the mirror. 'It can't be right for us to go on seeing each other while you're working on this case. What would the superintendent say if he knew?'

'O'Loughlin is always trying to marry me off to any woman he comes across,' he parried. 'I suppose he would be pretty annoyed if he found out about us. He would feel he should take me off the case and that wouldn't suit him at all. But that's his problem, not mine.'

'I don't think we should see each other again until this case is cleared up,' she insisted, holding his gaze in the mirror.

'You're tired of me already,' he teased her.

'No, Mitch. I don't think you'd wear out quickly.' She stood up and held him lightly by the shoulders. 'I don't want to start coming between you and your job. Anyway, I want you left on the case so you can nail the bastard who killed Brian.'

As she saw him discreetly out by the side door, she assured him, 'Don't worry, I'll be here when all this is over — if you haven't arrested me in the meantime.'

111

9

Michael McDevitt, the assistant registrar, was more co-operative than Mitchell had expected from their encounter on the previous day. Asked to produce the personnel files relating to the Genetics Department this morning, McDevitt's response had been a mixture of disbelief and horror—Mitchell wasn't sure whether this was a reaction to the notion of giving the police access to the university's records or to the prospect of having to come in on a Saturday morning. However, McDevitt, today as immaculately casual in mohair sweater and cavalry twill slacks as he had been impeccably formal in dark suit and club tie yesterday, was waiting when Mitchell and Sam Smith were shown into his office. Two trolleys flanked the desk, one bearing stacks of files in coloured covers, the other laid with cups and saucers.

'I hope you have everything that you need, gentlemen.' McDevitt waved a hand at the files with the satisfied air of a conjurer who has successfully accomplished a difficult trick. 'The blue files are academic staff, the pink are non-academic, and the buff are postgraduate students. You won't find much to interest you. We don't keep comprehensive data on our staff. Most of the files contain only the application documents submitted at the time of ap-

112

pointment, and financial details such as salary scales and pension arrangements.'

McDevitt breezed towards the door. 'Some coffee should materialise shortly, so make yourselves at home, gentlemen.'

Leaving Sam to read about the non-academic staff, Mitchell picked up the bundle of blue files and extracted Catherine Gildea's. It turned out to be typical of all the academics' files. Most of the items related to her application for her present job and told Mitchell little that he did not already know. Included was an enthusiastic letter of reference from Barry; and Mitchell found himself wondering if Catherine had ever come across a copy of that in Barry's desk. There was little else of interest, except some routine reports from Roche on her progress during her probationary years, and an application for promotion to senior lecturer, dated December of the previous year. Mitchell was impressed by the long list of publications appended to the application, the majority of which included Barry's name as a co-author. It was a substantial monument to the partnership, platonic or otherwise, of Gildea and Barry. Clipped to the application were formal letters of recommendation from Roche and Barry and a copy of a letter stating that the Senior Promotions Committee had approved her application.

As he worked his way alphabetically through the rest of the files, Mitchell found that they contained very similar material. Only when he came to Chris O'Mahony's did he find anything worth looking at a second time. O'Mahony had also applied for promotion the previous December. His application and list of publications were similar to Gildea's, and Mitchell was surprised to see that the application had been unsuccessful. He turned to the accompanying letters from Roche and Barry. Both said essentially the same thing: they praised O'Mahony's

113

teaching ability and research achievements, but regretted that the candidate lacked that sense of responsibility expected of a senior academic. Neither recommended his promotion, although Roche added, diplomatically, that he thought the application should be reconsidered in a year or two, "when Dr O'Mahony will be older and, perhaps, wiser".

As he put down the file, Mitchell wondered if it was significant that the seemingly transparent O'Mahony had omitted to mention that Barry's lack of approval had cost him his promotion.

The last file was that of Professor Roche. Except for some correspondence about pension arrangements, the most recent document was his application for the chair of genetics. Mitchell leafed through it without any great attention until he came to the final page, which was a summary of Roche's CV. It was a predictable account of the stages of development of a successful academic, except for one interlude from 1943 to 1946, when Roche had been a pilot officer in the RAF.

'Sam, we might have something interesting here.' Mitchell read the entry to the sergeant. 'I wonder what became of Roche's service revolver after he left the RAF. We'll go and have a word with him as soon as we get through these.'

* * *

The suburb where Bob Roche lived was a byword for middle-class comfort and affluence. His house was a solid prewar semi-detached in a quiet side-road.

'I'm sorry if we're keeping you from the match, professor.' Mitchell's apology was perfunctory. 'But I'm sure you appreciate the urgency of our enquiries.'

'I gave my ticket away yesterday, inspector. Two days ago I wouldn't have believed that anything could keep me from Lansdowne Road today, but I couldn't enjoy the game with this unfortunate business hanging over my department.'

He showed the two officers into his study. Like everything about Roche, the room was an exercise in understated good taste. It could have been an illustration of the professional man's study in *Homes and Gardens*. The Victorian solidity of leather-topped desk, wooden filing cabinet, ceiling-height bookshelves and hide upholstery was offset by Swedish desk-lamps, a cordless telephone and a desktop computer. The businesslike aura of the room was relieved by full-length windows that occupied most of one wall. The tweed curtains were drawn back to reveal a panoramic view of colourful flowerbeds with the wooded foothills of the Dublin Mountains in the distance.

Mitchell avoided the comfortable armchair indicated by the professor and chose instead the swivel-chair behind the desk, unwilling to give Roche any unnecessary psychological advantage during this interview. Smith sat down beside him.

'Do you own a gun, professor?' Mitchell forestalled further urbanities.

'No.' Taken by surprise, Roche was uncharacteristically direct. 'I used to do a bit of duck shooting, but sitting in damp hides on cold autumn mornings lost its magic for me several years ago. I sold my guns to a very respectable fellow from Walkinstown. I could find the receipt if you wanted it.'

'No, professor, that won't be necessary. It's not a shotgun we're talking about. How about something smaller — like a revolver?'

If Roche was perturbed, he didn't show it. He waited impassively for Mitchell to continue.

'What happened to your service revolver when you left

the RAF? We know that many ex-officers retained them as souvenirs — strictly against the law, of course. A blind eye was turned until 1969, when too many of them started falling into the wrong hands. Perhaps you handed yours in at that time?'

'No, unfortunately, I didn't.' Roche, for the first time, seemed less than sure of himself. 'I wish I had, because the damn thing was stolen, eventually.'

'Was it a Webley?'

Roche nodded.

'When was it stolen?'

'About two weeks ago.' Roche consulted his pocket diary, 'On the twenty-fourth of February, to be precise. The house was broken into and the gun disappeared along with my wife's chequebook, several pieces of jewellery, and some cash.'

'You reported this?'

'My wife called the gardai, of course, as soon as she came home and found we'd had a break-in. They came and took a list of the missing items. They thought they knew the culprits.'

'Good. The local station will be able to confirm the theft of your gun.'

'Well, no, actually, inspector.' Roche was almost stammering in his haste to explain. 'My wife didn't realise at the time that the gun had been taken. It was only later that I discovered it was missing, and — well, I didn't bother saying anything to the gardai then.' Roche lowered his voice conspiratorially. 'I hadn't got a licence and I was afraid there might have been a bit of a fuss.'

Mitchell refrained from comment, and, after a few moments, the implications began to dawn on Roche. 'Inspector, am I to infer that you think that the gun that killed Brian Barry might have been mine?'

'Barry was shot with a Webley .45,' Mitchell said

116

bluntly. 'The forensic evidence suggests that Barry did not shoot himself. Therefore we must establish ownership of the weapon. There are relatively few Webleys around, so it would not be surprising if the weapon turns out to be yours.' He looked up at Roche but the professor sat immobile, staring intently at his well-manicured finger-nails. 'Do you know the number of your gun?'

Roche got awkwardly to his feet and rooted through the filing cabinet. 'I have a note of it somewhere, inspector.' After much rummaging, he produced a page torn from a loose-leaf notebook. Mitchell glanced at the number. 'Yes, professor, that's the same gun.'

Roche subsided into his chair and looked in turn at the two policemen. 'You mean the blackguards who pinched my revolver also broke into the department and shot poor Brian?'

'There was no evidence of a break-in. However, your thief might have stolen a key to the department. Were any keys missing after your burglary?'

'No, we were very lucky,' Roche replied without hesi-tation. 'Both my wife and I had our keys with us that morning, so we were saved the expense of changing the locks.'

'There was no spare key to the department elsewhere in the house?'

'Positively not, inspector.' Roche's manner was still congratulatory.

'In that case, professor, we'll have to look for an alter-native connection with the department.'

Roche, who was not a stupid man, finally got the point. 'You don't believe my gun was stolen?'

'You said you didn't notice that your gun was gone until some time after the burglary.' Mitchell sidestepped the question. 'When did you miss it?'

'That night. I kept the gun in the cabinet beside the

bed. To be honest, now that my sons have left home and we're here on our own it gave me a sense of security. My wife was never happy about having it in the house, and on the night of the burglary she made some remark about how little use the gun had been in this instance. That reminded me to look, and I discovered it had been stolen.'

'How often did you check it?'

'Very infrequently.'

'Can you remember when you saw it last?'

'Not for two or three weeks,' Roche was becoming increasingly discomfited, 'but I can't say exactly.'

'So there's no evidence that it was taken by your burglars.' Mitchell allowed some seconds for this to sink in. 'Could any other member of your staff have known that you kept a gun in the house?'

'Inspector, you seem quite determined that either I or one of my colleagues shot poor Brian.' Roche was bristling with indignation.

Mitchell was unimpressed by this display of rancour, but he tried to be patient. 'Professor, good policemen, like good scientists, always look hardest at the least improbable explanation. Firstly,' he counted off the points on his fingers, 'almost all murders are committed by people who know their victim well. Secondly, the location of Barry's murder suggests a connection with your department. Now the murder weapon turns out to have belonged to a colleague.' Mitchell turned his hands, palms upwards, on the desk in a gesture of dispassion. 'So think carefully whether anybody from the department, other than yourself, might have known where you kept your gun.'

'As it happens, inspector, all of them knew.' Roche gave an audible sigh. Mitchell was uncertain whether it betrayed anxiety or relief. 'It's not something I would normally talk about but, because of a silly prank at a

118

party here last term, everybody found out about the gun.'

'What sort of prank?'

Roche looked embarrassed but reluctantly explained, 'Years ago I'd shown my revolver to one of my colleagues. He thought it would be amusing to pretend to hold up the other guests. He'd probably had rather too much to drink. He took the gun, got himself up in a leather jacket and a balaclava belonging to one of my sons, and slipped out the back door. He certainly fooled me when I answered the front door and he stood there pointing the gun at me and demanding money in a fake Belfast accent. It frightened the life out of everybody, particularly the ladies. Brian was very cross about it because the stupid ass didn't realise the gun was loaded, and there could easily have been a serious accident. After that, it was no secret that I owned a gun.'

'The culprit was Chris O'Mahony?'

'Really, inspector,' Roche remonstrated, 'I would prefer to let the perpetrator remain anonymous — but I suppose, under the circumstances, you will insist on the details.' He glared challengingly at Mitchell, but his curiosity was stronger than his reserve. 'How did you guess it was Chris?'

Mitchell tried not to look smug. 'I had intended asking you what O'Mahony had done to make both you and Professor Barry consider him unfit for promotion.'

'Yes, that was unfortunate,' Roche admitted. He looked thoughtfully at the two policemen. 'Chris is really quite a good lad,' he insisted. 'It was just his bad luck to have chosen Brian as his second referee. Worse luck, the requests for references landed on our desks the day after the party. I left the letter unanswered for a week, and by then I had cooled down sufficiently to have overlooked the whole silly business and written a decent recom-

119

mendation. However, Brian was implacable. Not only did he give Chris the thumbs down himself, but he insisted that I do so too. We had quite a heated argument about it, as a matter of fact.' Roche, who seemed to be rapidly regaining his normal composure, surprised Mitchell by admitting disarmingly, 'I suppose I finally gave in because I felt guilty about my own responsibility for the affair — contributory negligence, I suppose you people would call it.'

'Could O'Mahony have known about the bad references that you both gave him?' Sam Smith unexpectedly interrupted the professor's reflections.

'Yes, indeed, sergeant.' Roche swung round in his chair to face Smith. 'Barry told Chris to his face what he intended to say, and informed him that he had persuaded me to the same view.' He shook his head despairingly. 'He maintained it would be dishonourable to give a bad reference behind the candidate's back.'

Roche turned back to face Mitchell and wagged a didactic finger at him. 'The whole thing was very typical of Brian. He was normally very easygoing. Quite a perfectionist in his own work, but tolerant of others' shortcomings — up to the point where their mistakes might be harmful. Then he became unyielding. But he was always scrupulously fair,' he added aggressively, as if the inspector had put forward the opposing view. 'You or I, inspector, might find a way of coping with a problem without becoming too personally involved, but not Brian. He told Chris what he thought of him and what he intended to do about it.'

Mitchell lit a cigarette. He contemplated the flame of the match for some seconds before extinguishing it carefully. 'How did O'Mahony react to all this?'

'Oh, at first he was contrite. He'd made a complete ass of himself and probably welcomed a bit of penance. But

I think he became quite bitter about it afterwards and thought his punishment was excessive. It rubbed salt in his wounds when Catherine Gildea was promoted and he wasn't.'

'Would O'Mahony have had an opportunity to steal your gun before the burglary?' Mitchell put the question bluntly.

'Really, inspector!' Roche's face reddened and he stood up abruptly. He seemed genuinely angry. 'I must protest at the implications of that question.'

'I have to consider all possibilities.' Mitchell sounded detached. 'Was there any recent occasion on which O'Mahony might have had access to the gun.'

Roche threw himself into his chair and said wearily, 'My birthday was on the twenty-first of February. It is something of a tradition to have a party on my birthday. Anybody could have been in the bedroom that evening. Most of the coats were left there.'

'And O'Mahony was at the party?'

'Almost everybody from my department was there — staff and postgraduates,' Roche admitted reluctantly, but braced himself to protest again, 'Honestly, I can't bring myself to believe that one of my colleagues would have stolen my gun and murdered Brian.'

Mitchell grinned at him sourly. 'Try to believe it, professor. You would find my alternative theory even less attractive!'

10

'Powerful match!'

'Did you ever see such a try, man?'

Dignan's bar was full of jubliant red-and-white-scarved rugby supporters as Mitchell and Smith elbowed their way to the snug, where they found Superintendent O'Loughlin enjoying a quiet pint and a serious discussion of the shortcomings of the Irish front row with the white-aproned curate.

'It was a lousy match, lads. You were fortunate to be spared the spectacle of such national humiliation.' The superintendent downed the remains of his pint. 'We'd better go and order our steaks before the men of Harlech eat them all.'

'There'll be decent football tomorrow. We'll go to see Kerry beat Dublin in Croke Park,' Mitchell taunted his sergeant as they fought their way out of the snug.

The grill room was already busy but they found a relatively secluded table. Not until large T-bone steaks and fresh pints of Guinness had been set in front of them, and O'Loughlin had supplemented his litany of the faults of the Irish team with some uncharitable reflections on the parentage of the referee, was Mitchell allowed to recount the developments of the afternoon.

'Is Roche telling the truth?' O'Loughlin, who had been

eating steadily throughout Mitchell's report, put down his knife and fork and gave his undivided attention to the case.

'We've checked with the station in Kill o' the Grange,' Smith said. 'The house was burgled, but the job had all the hallmarks of local gurriers who are out on bail pending trial for a dozen similar offences. They're small-time operators; they usually take just cash and cheque cards, spirits, jewellery, videos — the sort of items that they can dispose of quickly.'

'I suppose there's always a market for guns,' Mitchell added, 'but if those lads took it, it's too much of a coincidence that it should turn up again in Roche's own department.'

'What do you make of Roche?'

'He's very plausible: polished on the surface but tough underneath. I'd say he would be cool enough to eliminate somebody who got in his way.' Mitchell speared a forkful of chips and chewed them thoughtfully. He shook his head. 'There's a history of hostility between Roche and Barry, but why should it ignite again after the best part of fifteen years, particularly now that Roche is nearly due to retire? He has an alibi for the whole of Thursday evening — but Sam is going to start dissecting that on Monday.'

'Where does all this leave us?'

'The break-in is a red herring. I think the gun was pinched from Roche's bedroom some time before the burglary,' Mitchell insisted, 'probably during the birthday party. Several possible suspects were there that night.'

'Such as?'

'Chris O'Mahony, for one. He's very immature, just the sort to harbour a grudge for a few months and then do something stupid, more or less on impulse. He has the same alibi as Roche for the night of the murder, so that's another job for you, Sam.'

'Yes, lads, it's essential now to find out exactly what went on at the Burlington.' O'Loughlin was marshalling his troops. 'Firstly, establish the minimum time it takes to get from there to the O'Meara Building and back. Then I want a detailed scrutiny of the whereabouts of all the people from the Genetics Department during that critical period. If the function that night was the usual sort of thing, with people moving about from one group to another, you'll have to interview everybody who was there and get them to recall who they talked to and when. It won't be easy,' he warned, resuming his normal pessimism.

O'Loughlin caught the waiter's eye and ordered more pints before turning his attention to the inspector. 'Now, Mitch, what about the lady in the case? Have you interviewed her again?'

'I spoke to Dr Gildea again last evening. You were right, sir. At one time she and Barry had something going. However, it's been over for years and now she's just a friend of the family, so to speak.'

'You believe her?'

'I think so, sir.' Mitchell tried to make it sound like a considered opinion. 'She was pretty frank about it. I feel she was telling the truth.'

'And you, sergeant,' O'Loughlin snapped. 'What was your impression?'

'I wasn't present, sir.' Smith was clearly thrown off balance by the question, but he fielded it deftly. 'I had to keep an eye on things in the O'Meara Building.'

'I see.' O'Loughlin eyed Mitchell knowingly. He seemed to be debating the wisdom of making any comment in front of Smith, when he was interrupted by a waiter summoning the inspector to the phone.

'Be a good lad, sergeant, and take the call.' He glanced

ominously at Mitchell. 'You can say the inspector is busy.'

'You're a fool, Mitchell,' O'Loughlin said as soon as the sergeant was out of earshot. The waiter chose this moment to take their plates, and the superintendent watched him impatiently while he cleared the table. Singing had started at a table beside them and Mitchell, slightly off key, joined enthusiastically in a chorus of "Bread of Heaven".

'Are you compromised with this woman — emotionally, I mean?' O'Loughlin cut across his choral efforts. 'I don't give a fiddler's if you've ridden the arse off her as long as she has no emotional hold over you.'

'You can trust me, sir.' Mitchell was surprised by his own detachment. 'I won't deny Gildea is an attractive woman, but you've no cause for anxiety about my judgment.'

Whatever retort O'Loughlin might have made was forestalled by the return of Sam Smith, who announced with scarcely suppressed excitement. 'That was Maureen Brennan, sir. Mrs Barry wasn't at the Bridge Club on Thursday evening.'

'Is she sure?' Mitchell, delighted by the distraction, asked eagerly. 'Mrs Barry admitted she wasn't playing, just watching the hands.'

'She talked to several people from the club,' Smith reported as he sat down. 'None of them remembers seeing Mrs Barry on Thursday night, so she got the address of the club secretary,' he said approvingly, willing to commend his colleague's thoroughness. 'According to the secretary, Mrs Barry only plays on Mondays. She'd have noticed if she was there on a Thursday. The man who looks after the bar is equally certain that Mrs Barry wasn't there that night.'

'Has Brennan asked Mrs Barry about this?' O'Loughlin asked.

125

'No, sir, that's why she phoned. She felt she should consult the inspector before doing anything further.' Smith, his duty done, took a long pull at his pint and wiped his mouth with the back of his hand.

'I'll phone her,' Mitchell promised. 'I'd like to be there when she puts this to Anna Barry.'

* * *

When Mitchell and Brennan arrived at the Barrys' house the following afternoon, the family were having an early tea in the sunny front room. Extra cups and saucers were brought in immediately and the two detectives found themselves sitting down to tea and cake.

'Afternoon tea on Sunday is something of a ritual in this house. We're trying to keep everything as normal as possible for the children this weekend,' the elder Mrs Barry explained as she pressed a second slice of fruit cake on Maureen Brennan. Already aggrieved at missing the game in Croke Park, Mitchell was getting increasingly irritated by his Sunday afternoon being wasted at a tea party, but he finally managed to detach Anna Barry from her family, on the pretext of examining the late professor's study.

Brian Barry's study, on the first floor, was as different in character from Bob Roche's as the two men themselves must have been. Although the room contained the same essential furnishings as Roche's study, the impression on the visitor was totally different. While Roche's sanctum spoke of a busy, methodical man, this room betrayed the late Brian Barry as never quite catching up with the paperwork. The study had obviously not been a success as a sanctuary from the family. Frequent incursions by the younger Barrys were evident from the trail of toy cars and moth-eaten teddy-bears between the stacks of books and papers, and a heap of knitting had been aban-

126

doned on the single battered armchair.

'We'd like a word with you, Mrs Barry.'

Picking up the knitting, Anna Barry sat down in the armchair. She absently rearranged the stitches while Mitchell leaned against the side of the desk facing her. Maureen Brennan removed a pile of books from a chair beside the window, and unobtrusively opened her notebook as she sat down.

'Mrs Barry, you know that we are now working on the assumption that your husband was murdered. In that context, we want to ask you some further questions. Miss Brennan will be making a note of your answers.' Mitchell paused to ensure that she fully understood what he meant.

Anna Barry nodded. 'It's about Thursday night, isn't it?'

'Where were you?'

'I was visiting a friend — in his flat,' she added, obviously anxious to avoid any ambiguity. 'I wanted to tell you — not just because I knew you'd find out eventually — but I couldn't say anything on Friday in front of Granny. I discussed the situation with my friend last night and he said I must tell you the truth immediately. He's been away, and that was my first opportunity to tell him what had happened.' She started to play with the knitting wool again.

To ease the tension, Mitchell slid from the desk and went to look out of the rather dusty window into the back garden. 'Just tell me where you were on Thursday evening and who you were with.'

'I'd like to tell you the whole story.'

Mitchell guessed that Anna, like Catherine, needed a confessor. He felt a twinge of resentment at being cast again in this role, but he shrugged and returned to his perch on the desk.

127

'I used to play bridge twice a week, on Mondays and Thursdays, until about eighteen months ago. Then I met a man.' She glanced up at Mitchell to see how he was reacting. He had picked up a small brass paperknife and was examining it minutely.

'Actually, I'd known him for ages.' Her pace was more confident. 'We're in the same political party and at first we used just go for a drink together after branch meetings. He's separated from his wife and is pretty lonely.

'One Thusday, he phoned and asked me to go to the Abbey with him that night to see *The Plough and the Stars*; we'd had an argument about O'Casey's politics a few nights earlier. As it happened, my bridge partner had flu that week, so I was able to accept. I had fully intended telling Brian, but, for some reason, he didn't come home for supper and Granny just assumed I was going to the bridge club. After that it somehow became a habit that Jim and I went somewhere together most Thursday nights, and I never got around to telling Brian.'

Absently, she inspected the piece of knitting, and picked up some stitches that had dropped from the end of one needle. Mitchell said nothing, giving her a chance to collect her thoughts.

'I won't pretend to be in love with Jim.' She spoke very quietly, and Mitchell was more aware of her Yorkshire accent than he had been earlier. 'He interests me a lot and he is totally different from Brian. He has a sort of ruthlessness that Brian lacked — not usually a very admirable quality but often attractive to women. I know it's a cliché, but I'm forty-one, I've been married eighteen years, and I suppose I found it reassuring that I was still interesting to someone other than my husband.'

She looked up at Mitchell, willing him to understand her position.

'Tell me about Thursday.'

'Jim had to go to Liverpool that night on the car ferry, so I just went to his flat and helped him pack. Then we went down to his local pub for a drink before he set off. I'd been home about half an hour when you and Catherine arrived.'

'My only concern is to know where you were that night — particularly around eight thirty.' Mitchell tried not to sound judgemental.

She looked startled but assured him, 'Jim and I were together all evening, from half past seven until nearly ten.' Then, realising that this was unlikely to be regarded as a satisfactory alibi, she added, 'We got to the pub about eight thirty. We had been there quite a while before the nine o'clock news came on.'

'Your friend will be able to confirm this? We'll need his name and address.'

Mitchell's eyebrows rose when she identified her friend. Not only was Jim Gannon a well-known and respected figure in the trade union movement, he was also a respected patron of Paddy Lynch's pub.

'Was it Lynch's you were in?'

'Yes. How did you know?'

'I know Jim fairly well myself, as it happens. I believe I've seen you with him in there the odd night, now that I think about it.' Mitchell looked at Anna Barry with a new interest, and couldn't resist asking her, 'Were you never afraid your husband would get to hear you were out drinking with Jim Gannon? It's a small town to be taking that sort of chance in.'

She shook her head confidently. 'Oh, Brian knew I sometimes went to Lynch's with Jim after party meetings — in the same way that he often took Catherine for a drink after work.' She paused. 'I sometimes wonder, am I as naïve about that relationship as Brian was about myself and Jim?' She looked searchingly at Mitchell. 'I expect you could tell me, inspector, but I definitely do not want to know.'

Mitchell made no comment, and she continued hurriedly, 'So it wouldn't have mattered if some kind person told Brian that I'd been in Lynch's with Jim.'

'You're sure your husband didn't suspect that you and Jim Gannon were more than friends?' Mitchell insisted. 'Couldn't that have explained his preoccupation in the last few months?'

'No, he didn't know.' She shook her head pensively. 'In a way, I almost hoped he'd find out.'

The ball of wool slipped from her grasp and rolled across the floor. Mitchell retrieved it and handed it back to her without comment. 'That sounds as if I wanted to hurt Brian,' she said sadly as she started to rewind the ball of wool, passing it forward and back through the tangled skein. 'I loved Brian but there were times when I wanted to shake some of the righteousness out of him. The shock of finding that I had been unfaithful to him would have wounded him deeply, but it might have made him more human.' Clearly startled by her own admission, Anna Barry started knitting with intense concentration, but tears were running down her face.

To let her regain composure, Mitchell started leafing through the papers on the desk.

'The professor must have brought a lot of work home with him,' he said absently.

Anna wiped her eyes with a tissue and tried to make her voice sound normal. 'Yes, he brought a huge briefcase of papers home with him every evening. Mind you, he didn't always get around to taking anything out of it.' She smiled wanly. 'I used to tell him that he had the best travelled papers in the college. He brought most of them back with him each morning, but even so, the piles here grew all the time.'

'Do you mind if I have a look through them?'

'No, I'll have to do something about them eventually.' She looked hopelessly at the mound of papers. 'I'm not able to face it yet.'

Mitchell took a cursory look though the documents piled on the desk, but most were photocopies of articles from journals and other scientific papers. There was nothing of interest among them. He tried the drawers of the heavy oak desk but found them locked.

'Have you a key for this?'

'No, Brian kept it on his key-ring.'

Mitchell examined the locks and concluded that they could not be forced without inflicting considerable damage on the desk. 'I'd like to have a look at what's inside. I suppose the professor kept his personal and financial papers here?'

'No, I think there's only stuff relating to his work. Brian was hopeless about money or business. I looked after the household finances, and those papers are in a bureau downstairs. I don't think there's anything important in that desk. He locked it just to stop the children playing with it.'

'I'll get a key for it during the week and have a look through it, if I may. To be on the safe side, I'd like to keep this room locked in the meantime.' He stood up and tried the handle of a door in the wall behind the desk. 'Where does this go?'

'Into a bathroom,' Anna Barry explained. 'We put in a bathroom off our bedroom and it seemed a good idea to have access from this room too, but we keep that door bolted from the inside all the time. Otherwise we'd never keep the kids out of it.'

Mitchell nodded and locked the door into the hall behind him, slipping the key into his pocket as he followed the two women from the room.

131

11

Roche looked from one to another of his six colleagues as they awkwardly resumed their seats after observing a minute's silence. His expression was a carefully modulated mixture of the solemn and the urbane. He waited pointedly to ensure undivided attention, before embarking on a tribute to Brian Barry and an ambiguous reference to 'the deeply disturbing' circumstances of his death.

'It will not be easy for this department to return to normal after what has happened. In addition to our emotional trauma, there are logistical problems. Inspector Mitchell intends to keep Brian's office locked and to restrict access to the building for some days.' Roche looked deliberately around the table to ensure that the implications of his remarks had sunk in.

He took a gold propelling pencil from his breast pocket and deliberately ticked the first item on a list on the table in front of him. 'Anna Barry phoned today to tell me that the coroner will release the remains on Wednesday. The burial will be on the following day. We will all wish to be present at that unhappy event and, as a mark of respect, I propose to cancel classes and to close the department for the day.' He made another tick on his list.

He went on to stress, at some length, the necessity of restoring calm, in view of the impending examinations, and the consequent urgency of reallocating Brian Barry's classes. 'Obviously I shall talk to the vice-chancellor, as soon as is seemly, about a replacement.' Perking up at the prospect of political manoeuvres, his voice became more brisk. 'However, we could not hope to make a new appointment before the autumn, and in the meantime we must do what we can with the resources available.'

He paused to register the significance of this, but resumed before anybody could interrupt.

'Catherine, I fear that you must bear the brunt of much of the extra work.' He smiled avuncularly at her. She failed to reciprocate this expression of goodwill, but then, to the disappointment of her colleagues, agreed without argument to take over Barry's lectures for the remainder of the year, as well as supervision of his three final-year students.

'Their reports are due to be handed in by the end of this month,' Roche reminded her as he ticked the third and fourth items on his list. Gildea just nodded.

'Now what about Brian's postgraduate students?' He looked enquiringly at her.

She said nothing. She seemed mesmerised by the length of the list in front of him.

A lesser man might have found her silence intimidating, but Roche was not so easily deterred. 'How many postgraduates was Brian directing?'

'There are two in their first year, one each in their second and third years, and of course, Jacky Whelan.' Her voice betrayed no emotion, but her foot was tapping menacingly on the carpet under the table. 'There's Gerry Flynn too, but he's a postdoctoral fellow.'

'Do you think you could cope with them, at least temporarily?' Roche did not sound sanguine.

133

'I have four of my own already.'

Roche gripped the edge of the table as if bracing himself for her refusal. A ripple of interest spread round the table in anticipation of conflict, but to everybody's surprise she conceded. 'One of mine is almost finished, so if I could off-load Brian's first-year students I might just manage. When Gerry Flynn comes back from Zürich he'll be able to help.'

'What is Flynn doing in Zürich?' Roche sounded annoyed. He disliked not knowing what was happening in his department.

'He has a visiting fellowship. Brian wanted him to learn something about synthetic polynucleotides.'

'When is he due to return?'

'The original plan was that he should go to Zürich for six months, starting in March, but Brian changed his mind and sent him off at the end of January. I don't know when he'll be finished there. I tried to phone him on Friday to tell him about Brian but he had taken a few days off and they didn't know where he'd gone.'

'Well, things should be easier for you when he's here.' Roche sounded relieved, almost cheerful. 'Now how about volunteers to supervise these two first years?' He beamed optimistically around the table, but five pairs of eyes were minutely examining its polished surface. 'What research are they doing at the moment, Catherine?'

'They are both working on RNA biosynthesis. Perhaps Conor could look after them,' she said mischievously. 'There must be a few unanswered questions arising from your recent discoveries about RNA, Conor, that they could follow up?'

'That sounds a very sensible idea.' Roche chose to ignore the waspishness in her question. 'How about it, Conor?'

'Really, Bob, you know I'd like to help, particularly in

134

view of my great esteem for Brian, but I do not intend to pursue that aspect of my work any further. There are so many other interesting topics demanding attention.' Dodd took off his spectacles and massaged the bridge of his nose. 'For instance, Catherine,' he peered myopically at her, 'if either of your young people would like to work on cell walls, I would be delighted to take them on; but if they want to work on RNA you'd better look after them yourself.'

She looked annoyed but, before she could reply, Roche hastily intervened, 'Catherine, why don't you talk to the students and assess the situation?' He seemed anxious that the topic shouldn't become contentious. 'We'll discuss this again next week. Needless to say, if there is any way that I can help I would be only too happy. But you would be the first to agree', he gave a complacent smile, 'that I am quite ignorant of molecular biology.'

'Actually, Bob, you could take some of my lectures.' Gildea winked across the table at Colette Lalor, who was silently applauding her efforts. 'They have nothing to do with molecular biology,' she assured him. 'Tomorrow I'm supposed to start lecturing on the genetics of plant pathogens —as my share of Pat McIvor's teaching while he's away. I know nothing about the subject and haven't had time to do much reading about it. Perhaps you could take those, Bob?'

Roche was quite unnerved by this suggestion. 'I'm afraid I've got a bit out of touch with fungal genetics. Anyway, I'm pretty tied up with this new committee on environmental genetic hazards — trips to Brussels and so forth. I think, since you've started preparing the course, you'd better see it through. Unless, of course, anybody else would like to volunteer.'

Conor Dodd shook his head austerely. David Morgan looked embarrassed and muttered, 'Sorry, Catherine.'

Chris O'Mahony glanced up from putting the finishing touches to a doodle of a bespectacled cigar-smoking rabbit. 'Not my bag, Bob,' he said offhandedly. Paul Mooney and Colette Lalor looked at each other but avoided Roche's eye.

As the silence persisted, Roche hurriedly adjourned the meeting. The others gathered up their papers and began to file out of the room, but Roche called Catherine Gildea back.

'Catherine, dear,' he grasped her confidingly by the elbow, 'I'm sorry about those lectures. Muddle through with them as best you can. If you can't cope, just cancel the course. We can make it up next year.'

She edged towards the door, but hadn't escaped before he added, 'There's just one other small thing. I'm extern examiner for a master's thesis. I'm afraid some of the subject matter is a little beyond my ken and I had intended asking Brian to look at it for me. Perhaps you would be good enough to glance through it, and let me know whether it's up to scratch?'

* * *

Catherine Gildea hitched herself up onto a bench and looked at the students, who were sitting on high stools around the laboratory. They seemed ill-at-ease. They were unfamiliar with death and were uncertain how to comport themselves in its shadow.

'I'm not going to indulge in a panegyric,' she assured them. She was as good as her word. She devoted exactly three minutes to acknowledging Barry's contribution to his subject and his love for students. 'The best tribute we can pay him is to try to carry on the work he started.'

She looked around the group. 'I will help you as much as I can. However, there is an alternative.' She relayed Conor Dodd's proposal.

'He needn't worry about anybody taking him up on that offer,' Jacky Whelan commented in her most knowing voice.

'For most of you, the only option is to continue under my supervision.' Gildea raised her voice slightly but otherwise ignored Jacky's intervention. 'I'll have to look at your research notebooks so that I can become familiar with your projects.'

She slid down from the bench. 'Jacky, I've got to see Brian's fourth-year students. Would you collect everybody's notebooks, including Gerry Flynn's, and take them up to my office? I'd like a word with you, so please wait there until I get back.'

* * *

Two of the undergraduates had neatly typed reports ready to be handed in. Catherine Gildea happily dismissed them and turned her attention to Barry's remaining student. Peter McCormack had ostentatiously begun to wash some glassware while she had been talking to his classmates.

'You're having problems with your project, Peter?' She drew a stool up close to the sink. 'You'd better tell me about it.'

'Do you know what cAMP is, Dr Gildea?' McCormack didn't look up from his task.

'Yes, I know about cyclic adenosine monophosphate. Is that what your project is about?'

'Last October, the prof suggested that I should study the correlation between levels of cAMP and RNA at different growth rates. It seemed straightforward.' McCormack turned to face her, punctuating his remarks by brandishing a bottle-brush. 'The only problem was measuring cAMP. It's quite a tricky assay, but by the end of October I was getting reproducible results.' McCormack's face brightened momentarily. 'I think it was better than the prof expected from an undergraduate.'

Gildea nodded encouragingly, and unobtrusively wiped away the drops of water he had splattered over her.

'The prof was in Germany for two weeks in December, but I was so geared up about the project that I worked very hard while he was away. I did the experiments he had suggested and the results were really neat. They worked exactly as he predicted. Then I started wondering about cause and effect, and I set up some experiments to test this. I was sure that the level of cAMP would always be inversely proportional to the growth rate.' Fully caught up in his story now, McCormack abandoned the washing-up, dried his hands and pulled up a stool facing Gildea. 'When I did the first experiments I couldn't believe the results: the cAMP level was the same in all my cultures! I thought I had made a mistake and repeated everything twice, but I kept getting the wrong result.'

Gildea shook her head. 'There's no such thing as a wrong result, Peter. If that's what you found, then that's the result.'

'That's what I thought,' McCormack said eagerly. 'Even though I was disappointed that the results didn't fit my theory, I was very excited. When the prof got back, I couldn't wait to tell him. He was frightfully busy, so he wasn't really listening to me, but he was encouraging in an abstracted sort of way.' He grinned complicitously. 'You know how he was when he hadn't time to talk to you but was afraid you'd be offended if he rushed away.'

Gildea nodded. She knew only too well.

'He promised to look at my notebook during the vacation and I came back after Christmas thinking my project was finished, but I got an awful 'and when I saw the prof. He was quite unpleasant to me, said my results couldn't possibly be right and almost accused me of making them up. Then he calmed down and said it was a difficult assay and I must have made an error, or hadn't controlled the variables properly. I suggested doing the experiments again. He got really mad then and said I wasn't to do anything of the sort, and gave me a lecture on the cost of materials. It wasn't like him to be so cross; he could be sarcastic, but never angry like this.'

'You were very silly, Peter, to waste a lot of time and materials without checking that your experimental design was correct.' Gildea loyally reinforced her late colleague's verdict. 'Now you'd better tell me what you've been doing since then.'

'The prof suggested that, since I'd spent so much time developing the assay, I should measure cAMP in different species of fungi – it would be interesting and nobody seemed to have done it. It didn't sound very interesting, and I nearly said that this might be why nobody had bothered.' McCormack glared challengingly at her, but then added meekly, 'I thought I'd better keep my mouth shut and do what I was told.'

Gildea had difficulty keeping a straight face. 'That was a good idea,' she agreed dryly.

'Honestly, Dr Gildea, it wasn't such a bright idea.' He stood up, hands jammed in the pockets of his white coat. 'It wasn't a success. The cAMP assays were all right, but getting the bugs to grow was a pain.'

'Fungi can be difficult,' she said sympathetically.

'They're not difficult, they're impossible! They grow happily on the wallpaper, rugby boots and strawberry jam — everywhere except on the culture medium you've spent hours making up for them.'

Gildea laughed. 'Never mind, Peter. The important thing now is your report.'

'I have a few results, but they're not very reproducible. I suppose if I left out some of the duplicates, they might look okay.'

'Peter!' Gildea was outraged. 'Don't let me hear you mention doctoring results. If I think for one minute that you've fiddled any data, I'll make sure you fail your year's work.' She looked him in the eye, then said more equably, 'Now, let's see what you have.'

'There isn't very much.' He handed her his notebook. She flicked though it. 'No, there certainly isn't!'

'That's only what I've done since Christmas. I haven't worked very hard this term,' he admitted with disarming frankness.

'You must have been working hard recently. Wasn't it because you wanted to work late that the prof was here on the night he was killed?'

Peter looked at her uncertainly. 'That's the funny thing, Dr Gildea. I didn't often work late, not since Christmas, but the prof told me on Thursday morning that he'd be here that night if I wanted to stay on. I didn't want to, but I thought it would be diplomatic to take up the offer.'

Gildea said quickly, 'Give me your other notebook, the one you had in the Michaelmas term. Maybe we can patch your results together into something coherent.'

'The prof didn't return my other notebook.' He was looking sullen again.

'Don't worry. It must be in his office. I'll ask the police if I can get it.' She stood up to indicate the end of the subject. 'It's not like the prof not to give it back. He was usually meticulous about returning other people's notes.'

'I asked him for it a couple of times but he kept saying he'd brought it home and forgotten to bring it back,' McCormack muttered petulantly, but Gildea had moved to the other end of the laboratory and was gathering up her papers, not giving him her full attention. 'I don't

140

believe he ever intended giving it back to me,' he suddenly blurted out.

'What?' Gildea turned swiftly to face the student.

'I'm sorry, Dr Gildea.' McCormack picked up a length of rubber tubing from the bench and started winding it round his fingers, not looking at her. 'It sounds shabby now that the prof's dead, but I'm convinced he really found my results very interesting.' He gripped the tubing, and his knuckles showed white with tension. Looking Gildea in the eye, he said with deliberation, 'He didn't return my notebook because he and Gerry Flynn planned to publish those results, as soon as I had graduated.'

'Peter, that's an outrageous accusation!' Gildea gave full vent to her anger. 'You mustn't make allegations like that without evidence.'

McCormack threw the piece of tubing onto the bench. It bounced and fell on the floor at her feet, but they both ignored it. 'Ask Jacky if you don't believe me.' Shaken by the violence of Gildea's reaction, McCormack was on the defensive. 'She let it slip one day that Gerry had repeated all my experiments before he went to Zürich. How do you explain that?'

'There could be several explanations.' Gildea made it clear that she didn't intend to discuss the matter further, and moved to the door. 'You know as well as I do that Jacky isn't always the most reliable source of information. Your theory doesn't make sense.' Her anger had abated and she sounded puzzled. 'If the prof wanted to publish your results, he'd simply have written a paper with both your names on it.'

*   *   *

Talking to Peter McCormack had taken longer than Gildea had expected and she was surprised to find Jacky Whelan still waiting in her office. Jacky was sitting with her shoulders slumped on the desk and her head resting on her arms. The office was an exact replica of Brian Barry's room on the floor below, and the sight of Jacky sprawled across the desk was a startling reminder of the night of his murder.

However, it was soon obvious that Jacky was very much alive. At the sound of footsteps she straightened herself, but didn't turn her head.

'Sorry I was so long,' Gildea apologised breezily as she dumped her papers on the shelf behind the door. 'I'm glad you were able to take a nap.'

Receiving no response, Gildea turned and saw that the student's shoulders were trembling and, despite an obvious effort to regain control, her body was periodically shaken by huge sobs.

'Jacky, dear, what's the matter?'

Tearful students were not entirely a novelty to her, but they were usually delinquent first years; she had little experience of dealing with a distraught 25-year-old.

'I'm sorry,' Jacky Whelan managed to articulate, 'I didn't mean to cry.'

'Don't overdo it, Jacky, or you'll reduce me to tears as well.'

The prospect of a weeping lecturer seemed to unnerve Jacky so much that her sobbing stopped and she turned to stare at Catherine Gildea, her eyes still large with tears. 'It's just Brian's death,' she muttered incoherently.

'It must be a delayed reaction.' Gildea was tart. 'By all accounts you were in sparkling form in the bar on Friday night, despite the recent death of your supervisor.'

Jacky blushed. 'Who told you that? I suppose it must have been that dishy policeman.' Belatedly reacting to Gildea's asperity, she added sheepishly, 'I'm sorry, I might have been a bit indiscreet about you and Brian.

Did he say anything about that?'

'"Indiscreet" is not the word I'd use. "Imaginative" would be more appropriate. As a result, your nice policeman asked me some searching questions about my relationship with Brian.'

'Oh God, Catherine, I'm sorry! I wish I could learn to keep my big mouth shut, particularly when I've had a few jars.'

She looked genuinely contrite and Gildea relented. 'Never mind. There's no harm done. The questions were so obvious, they would have been asked sooner or later.' This seemed to be no consolation to Jacky, who started to cry again. 'It's not just Brian's death that's upsetting you, Jacky, is it?' Gildea insisted.

'Oh, it's that . . . ' Jacky let the sentence trail off 'and other things.'

'Such as?'

'My work is a mess.'

'Listen, Jacky, you're no Marie Curie, and, frankly, I can't see you pursuing a career as a researcher.' Gildea sat down beside her at the desk. 'However, you are highly intelligent and I'm sure that, if you put your mind to it, you'll be able to produce quite a decent thesis.'

'Do you really think so?' The student brightened perceptibly.

'We'll manage something,' Gildea said with more confidence than was justified. 'Gerry will be back soon. He's quite an expert in your field.'

What had seemed a happy afterthought to Gildea had the disconcerting effect of reducing the hapless student to further tears. However, this time she made an effort to overcome them, blowing her nose loudly on a rather grubby handkerchief.

'I wasted a lot of time in my first three years,' she confessed. 'But last year I worked hard and Gerry gave me a lot of help. God knows, poor Brian had tried but he'd given me up as a bad job. I don't blame him, but I can't understand why the same thing happened with Gerry.'

Jacky Whelan's voice faltered and, to forestall further tears, Gildea interjected briskly, 'He lost interest in what you were doing?'

'It was worse than that. After Christmas, Gerry suddenly seemed so busy that he never had time to talk. It wasn't like him. Before that, he used to describe his work to me in detail. He said he hoped I'd learn something from it — which, incidentally, I did — but actually he just loved talking and I was a captive audience.' Whelan hesitated. 'I don't know if you heard that Gerry and I share a flat,' she asked artlessly, as if afraid of shocking the older woman.

'I think somebody mentioned it.' The progress of that affair had been the subject of loud and ribald comment among Gildea's students throughout the Michaelmas term.

'That made everything worse,' Jacky continued, relieved to have crossed that hurdle. 'Gerry and I were together twenty-four hours a day. He refused to talk about the lab, so we talked about the weather, and eventually not even that.'

'What was Gerry working on that preoccupied him so much?'

'Obviously I don't know, since he refused to talk to me about it,' Whelan replied, a little too quickly.

'You must know something,' Catherine Gildea almost pleaded. When the student shook her head and maintained a stubborn silence, Gildea resorted to sarcasm. 'You invented the story you told Peter McCormack?'

Whelan looked abashed. 'I shouldn't have said anything, I suppose.' She dabbed at her eyes again but her tears were over. 'I told Peter not to repeat what I said to anyone.' She stood up and edged defensively towards the door.

Gildea laid a hand on her sleeve to detain her. 'Why did you think that Gerry was trying to reproduce Peter's results?'

'I managed to peek in Gerry's notebook. He caught me at it and was very cross, but I couldn't resist trying to find out what all the mystery was about. It was very disappointing really. Just masses of experiments measuring cyclic AMP. I expected something a bit more exciting.'

Gildea forbore to enquire what lurid experiments Jacky had imagined. 'Well, I'll be able to satisfy your curiosity tomorrow if I get time to look at Gerry's notebooks tonight.'

'There was only one notebook in Gerry's desk, and that was the one he was using last term.' Whelan sounded aggrieved. 'The recent one must be in Brian's office.'

'It can wait till tomorrow.' Gildea was resigned. 'There's a notebook of Peter's there too; I hope your "dishy" inspector will let me get them. I suppose Gerry's notebook is there. He wouldn't have left it in your flat?'

'Hardly likely, if he wanted to keep it secret,' Jacky unblushingly conceded.

* * *

An hour later, Catherine Gildea met Bob Roche as she emerged from the library laden with books. He insisted on carrying them to her car. 'My dear, I do hope you are not overdoing things,' he asked solicitously. 'We've all had quite a shock, you know. You should take a little rest and give yourself time to recover.'

'Don't worry, Bob, I'm just doing a little light reading on plant pathogens.'

Roche was unabashed. 'Perhaps exploring a new subject will divert you, take your mind off poor Brian.'

145

'I doubt it. There seems to be no escaping the subject, even in the library. I was looking for one of the classical papers on virulence in the *Journal of Microbiology* of 1964. Inevitably, the volume I wanted wasn't on the shelves and I found that Brian had borrowed it. I'll have to ask Inspector Mitchell if I can get it from his office.'

'I'm sure that shouldn't be a problem, Catherine. He seems a very civil sort of chap.'

* * *

Sitting by the fire in her study, Catherine Gildea was reading an article about the life cycle of the potato blight fungus. For the third time she pushed away the cat which was sitting on the journal and went back to read the opening paragraphs again. She wasn't concentrating. Each time her eyes had faithfully progressed down the page, but not a single fact about *Phytoptera* had registered in her brain.

Finally, she started taking notes, and for a while, managed to forget her anxieties. When the phone rang, she glanced at her watch, and was startled to discover it was already ten thirty.

'Any chance you'd take a thirsty policeman out for a drink after his hard day's work?'

'Do you realise what time it is, Mitch?'

'There's still time for a few scoops, if we go to Lynch's.'

'No. I'm not finished my day's work yet. I'll be burning the midnight oil as it is, without swanning off for a jar with you in the middle of it.'

'Why are you so busy? I thought only coppers had to work till this hour of the night.'

'It's my own fault. I'm preparing a lecture for nine o'clock tomorrow, on a subject I know nothing about. Of course I've known about these lectures since Christmas and intended to prepare them well in advance, but there was always something more urgent on the agenda. I should have done them at the weekend but, what with one thing and another, I wasn't up to intellectual activity.'

'Can't you cancel the lecture?'

'No. It's a point of honour to keep the show on the road. Anyway, I've almost finished preparing it now. But' she added hastily, 'I've still got a thesis to read before I go to bed.'

'How long is a thesis?'

'Fortunately, this one isn't very long. There are no experimental data to conflict with the theories.'

'I thought you scientists could never prove anything without masses of graphs and tables.'

She laughed. 'That's usually so, but this student lost all his experimental notebooks when the laboratories in Cork went on fire last year. He quotes his results from memory and I have to take them on trust.'

'Isn't that asking too great a suspension of disbelief?'

'Yes, it is, but I'll probably recommend that he be let through. Otherwise the poor little devil will have to start again from scratch. It would be good enough for him. I'm tired telling students to keep copies of important results, but of course they never do. By the way, speaking of notebooks, may I use my key to get into Brian's office, or is it still out of bounds? I need to get a journal and some notebooks from there.'

'Actually,' he was hesitant, 'I'd like you to go through some of Barry's papers with me tomorrow, if it wouldn't be too painful for you. I've had a superficial look but it's all Greek to me.'

'All right. I'll give you a hand after my lecture, if I can get the things I need at the same time.'

12

Mitchell was already in a bad mood by the time he reached his office in the Administration Building on Tuesday morning. Frustrated by Catherine Gildea's refusal to see him the night before, he had gone to Lynch's 'for one pint before closing time', but had still been there with a few of his cronies when Paddy Lynch had finished cashing up at two o'clock. As a result, he now felt far from well: his eyeballs ached, his head was thick, and a punitively vigorous toothbrush had failed to remove the taste of stale stout from his palate. He had overslept and had had no breakfast. After blearily making a pot of tea, he had realised that, because of his defection to Lynch's, he had forgotten to buy milk the night before.

Late leaving home, he got caught in the rush hour traffic. In an attempt to assuage his impatience, he turned on the car radio to listen to the sports report. Yet another biased and misinformed analysis of Kerry's disappointing performance in Sunday's game did nothing to improve his temper. He left the radio on but stopped listening in the middle of an interview with the Minister for Labour about youth employment schemes.

Stuck in a particularly intractable traffic jam in

Ranelagh, he became conscious of Donal O'Loughlin's gravelly Donegal accent. The interviewer was pressing for details of the investigation of what she referred to as 'the cold-blooded murder of a greatly respected academic'. The superintendent was skilfully parrying her questions with noncommittal responses about 'definite lines of enquiry'. However, the interviewer, obviously growing as impatient of O'Loughlin's equivocation as Mitchell often did himself, terminated the interview by suggesting growing public concern over security on the campus. With an oath, Mitchell extended a hand to silence the radio but realised that the item was not over. An interview with a county councillor followed, in which the councillor deplored the growing incidence of crime on campus, attributing it to police slackness on drugs, to cuts in spending on higher education, and to increasing permissiveness on the part of the university authorities. Mitchell switched him off in mid-sentence and turned his mind to the day ahead.

He disliked this stage of a case at the best of times. Once the first forty-eight hours had elapsed without an arrest, or at least the emergence of an obvious suspect, a case was rarely simple. Progress now would depend on paperwork, on sifting and cross-checking, on discovering an anomaly in a statement, a flaw in an alibi. He hated that sort of task. The only satisfaction to be derived from it was the pleasure of inflicting it on subordinates. Sam Smith denied him even that small gratification. The sergeant positively relished this sort of operation and regarded it as a challenge.

Mitchell's eventual arrival at the college coincided with the influx of students for nine o'clock lectures. Coming along the main road, he found himself assailed by aggressive cyclists who, in his current state of post-alcoholic paranoia, seemed to be deliberately aiming at him. When he reached the office there was no sign of tea. The kettle and the teapot lay dormant on a shelf, while Sam Smith, frowning with concentration, was busy taping large sheets of paper together, edge to edge, to form charts which he was pinning to the wall.

'Did you hear that gobshite on the radio?' Mitchell demanded as he dumped briefcase and anorak on a desk.

The sergeant muttered a greeting, but did not look up from his task.

'For God's sake, Sam, what are you doing?' Mitchell picked up the kettle. It was cold and it was empty.

Smith stood back to admire his handiwork. Mitchell, kettle in hand on his way to the door, looked over his shoulder. Each chart was neatly ruled with vertical and horizontal lines, dividing it into boxes.

'It's a timetable for checking the movements of all our suspects around the material time. Look, sir, this one is for the academic staff.' The sergeant pointed to the smallest chart. 'Each line down is a member of the staff and each row across is an interval of ten minutes between half past seven and half past eight on Thursday evening. For instance,' he ran his finger down the first column, 'this is Conor Dodd; everybody agrees that his lecture didn't end before eight o'clock, and Professor Roche said he was talking to him for a few minutes afterwards, so we can probably say that he is accounted for until ten past eight.' He pencilled an entry on the chart and drew neatly hatched lines with a ruler through the first four squares. 'I thought it would be easier if we could see, at a glance, where everybody was at any particular time.'

Mitchell sourly examined the charts, while Smith, without comment, removed the kettle from his grasp and went to fill it.

'What's the critical time, would you say?' Mitchell asked as Smith was plugging in the kettle.

'I tried it myself at eight o'clock last night, sir. It took me just under eleven minutes to drive here from the Burlington, but I might have been lucky. I only encountered one red light. Add, say, four minutes at either end as a generous estimate and our client would have to have left the hotel before a quarter past.'

'Just when the sherry was starting.' Mitchell nodded. 'Very convenient!'

'I've made out a form, sir.' Smith picked up a sheet of paper from a stack on the desk. 'I'm asking each guest to state who they were talking to and who was standing near them during the sherry party.'

Mitchell stared vacantly at the charts. They made his headache feel worse, and he thought of asking Smith to find him an aspirin, but he couldn't face the smug solicitude that this admission of suffering would elicit from the sergeant. Nevertheless Smith must have noticed his indisposition, because the tea was very strong and sweet. Mitchell indulged himself by allowing his mind to become completely blank while he gulped his tea, until he realised that the sergeant was trying to regain his attention.

'From the Carraig in Blackrock, sir, it would take about the same time by car, and probably a bit faster by motorbike or even by pushbike.'

'Sam, do you honestly think it could have been a student — even one as old as Jacky Whelan?'

'That's the bossy one with the earrings, isn't it, sir? Well, she's in the clear anyway. She was in Dun Laoghaire from four o'clock on Thursday afternoon with the bride's two cousins, organising everyone and everything from the sound of it.' Smith took the mug from the inspector's hand and refilled it with tea, stirring in the milk and sugar thoroughly. 'No, I think you're right, sir. I can't see it being a student.'

The sweet liquid was restoring Mitchell and the charts were coming back into focus. He studied them in turn. 'This is the one.' He prodded the list of academic staff with his index finger. 'I'll swear it's one of these seven, Sam.'

'Any chance you'll be interviewing Dr Gildea or Dr Morgan again, sir?' The sergeant asked hopefully.

'I'm seeing Dr Gildea this morning, as it happens, Sam,' Mitchell said warily. 'She's going to look at Barry's papers with me. Is there something you want me to ask her?'

'I just thought you might find out exactly where she and Dr Morgan were between half past seven and half past eight on Thursday.' He looked fervently at his charts. 'Just for completeness, like, sir.'

'All right, Sam,' Mitchell humoured him. 'I'll ask her, and I can drop in to see Dr Morgan too on my way to Barry's office.'

'By the way, the report on the office came over from the Technical Bureau. It's on your desk, sir.'

Mitchell pulled himself out of his trance-like fixation with the charts and sat down at his desk to slit open the brown envelope. He grimaced as he scanned the report. 'The only clear prints are Barry's and Gildea's,' he relayed the contents to the sergeant. 'Smudgy prints all over the room, as you might expect, including some on the desk drawers, which are tentatively identified as Ms J. Whelan's.' He laughed and explained to Smith about Jacky's nightly raids on her supervisor's correspondence.

* * *

'How did the lecture go?' Mitchell looked up from his silent contemplation of Barry's desk as Catherine Gildea appeared at the door.

'Not so badly, considering everything.' Wearing a

152

white coat again, and with her hair neatly pinned back, she looked very cool and distant.

'How is sleuthing?' she asked brightly, but her voice was brittle and her cheerfulness seemed forced. She made no move to enter the office but stood awkwardly in the doorway.

Mitchell felt uncomfortable and wished his head was clearer. He thought she was finding it difficult to adjust to their changed relationship, but then he realised that she was scarcely aware of his presence in the office. Her attention was focused on the desk, and it dawned on him that this was the first time that she had seen the room since Thursday night, when Barry's body had been slumped across it.

'I'm sorry, this can't be easy for you,' he said quietly in an attempt to regain her attention.

'It's not,' she replied tersely, 'but it had to happen sooner or later. I can't go through the rest of my life avoiding this room.' She stepped purposefully across the threshold and looked deliberately around the office.

In the bright morning light there was nothing threatening or sinister about the room. Mitchell said as much to her.

'I know, that's the worst thing. Everything looks so normal, I can't help expecting Brian to walk in at any minute.'

Mitchell stood up. 'Let's find those notebooks. Are they important?'

While she leafed through a row of notebooks on the shelf beside the desk, Gildea explained her problems with Peter's project and the difficulty of getting in touch with Gerry Flynn.

'I've asked the Zürich police to try to contact him; perhaps they'll be more successful,' Mitchell offered helpfully.

Gildea looked up in surprise. 'To let Gerry know about Brian? That was kind of you.'

'I need to be sure where he was on Thursday night.'

'You're very thorough' was all she said as she returned her attention to the bookshelves, but he registered her shock.

'They're not here,' she said finally. 'They might be locked in one of the drawers or in the filing cabinet. I have spare keys upstairs if you don't mind my opening them.'

'I have Barry's own key-ring here. It was in his pocket,' he said flatly, to forestall her inevitable question. 'Have you keys for all the locks here?' he asked as he tried several keys in the desk before finding the right one.

'Yes, I often needed papers from here in the evenings after Brian had gone home, so he gave me keys to everything.'

Both filing cabinets and all the drawers of the desk were crammed with papers and notebooks, but after ten minutes' searching, Gildea gave up in despair.

'Is this the only place they could be?'

'They could be anywhere, but Jacky was sure Gerry's notebook would be here.' She sounded despondent, but added facetiously, 'Of course, as I frequently point out to others, including yourself, Jacky is not a reliable source of information.'

Mitchell ignored her sarcasm and said briskly, 'Now, I'm afraid you're going to have to pay for being allowed hunt for your notebooks.' He indicated the papers on Barry's desk. 'I've had a quick look at them, but you might spot something to give us a clue to what was on Barry's mind the night he died.'

Seeing the look of dismay on her face, he added hurriedly, 'Just look at the recent correspondence and any notes that he might have made in the last week or so.'

He sensed that Gildea found being in the office

unpleasant but she visibly pulled herself together. 'Anything recent, which in this instance means from the current academic year, is likely to be here.' She pointed to the large card-board carton on the desk. 'Brian hated paperwork and always hoped that if he ignored it, it might go away.'

She started to inspect the items at the top of the box. 'Form for annual renewal of library ticket; notice of term dinner; subscription due to the Genetical Society; ditto the Royal Dublin Society.' She lapsed into silence and sorted methodically through the papers.

Halfway down she threw up her hands in despair. 'This is endless but it's all junk.'

'Yes, it looks like bumf,' Mitchell agreed. 'It's the same in any large organisation with photocopying facilities and an internal mail system. If they had to pay postage for all that, nine-tenths of it would disappear. Even so, I'd be grateful if you'd go through the rest of it in case I missed anything. Be careful to keep the stuff in order: we might need to refer to it later.'

'You can't have been too careful when you went through it yourself. It's all out of sequence now.'

Mitchell laughed. 'My dear woman, how could you possibly tell what order it should be in?'

'Chronologically, the stuff is all over the place. Look at the letters on top: they date from October. The next layer, these notices about computer courses, are dated November.' She leafed rapidly through the box. 'The whole stack has been more or less inverted, with the recent correspondence at the bottom.'

'Yes, I noticed that, but I didn't put any store by it, seeing what a jumble the whole room is in. But I'll have you know that, as a well-trained copper, I left those papers exactly as I found them.'

'Well, Brian never left them that way.' She was adamant. 'Like most seemingly disorganised people, he had little quirks of method. One memorable time, before I became familiar with this idiosyncrasy, I was looking for a missing manuscript, and put everything back in any old order. Well, the telling off I got! Ever since, I approached the box with the caution of an archaeologist, terrified of disturbing the stratification.'

Nearly another hour spent going systematically through the contents of the desk and the filing cabinets failed to unearth anything of interest. 'I'm sorry. I haven't been much help to you, or to myself.' She sounded defeated.

Mitchell looked at his watch. 'Would you have time for something to eat?'

'Yes, that would be nice. I'll get my jacket.'

He hesitated, embarrassed, and added, in an attempt to sound casual, 'Sit down for a minute first. I want to ask you a few questions.'

She looked put out, but shrugged off her annoyance and tried to appear relaxed as she sat down in the chair beside the desk.

'It's about Thursday,' he began. He took the other chair and placed it beside hers but didn't sit down, preferring to pace up and down the tiny room. 'Tell me again what you did on Thursday evening.'

She sighed theatrically. 'I went to tea in the restaurant with Owen and Maeve. We came back at about half past seven. I saw a light here in Brian's office, so I called in on the way up to my room. The rest you know.'

'What did you talk about?'

'I don't remember. Brian was busy. I could see he wanted me to go away, so I went away.' She sounded as if she was reciting a lesson learned by heart.

'Catherine, this is very important. You were the last person to talk to Barry. Please try to think back.' He sat down in the chair beside her at the desk. 'Pretend I'm Barry. Go out and come in again and try to reconstruct the conversation.'

She made a long-suffering face, but did as he asked without argument. 'Oh, Brian, I didn't expect to find you here,' she said with a false brightness. 'I saw the light on and thought the students had forgotten to turn it out.' Her face was expressionless but her eyes were hostile.

'Where was Barry sitting?' Mitchell asked quietly, ignoring her histrionics.

'At the desk.'

'What was he doing?'

'Sitting at the desk.'

'What was on the desk?' Mitchell resolved not to be impatient.

'The usual clutter, I suppose,' she answered off-handedly.

'Where exactly was he sitting?'

'More or less where you are now, but nearer the centre.'

'And the other chair?'

'Over in the corner, where it usually was. There were books and files on it.'

'Did you sit on it?'

'No, I didn't bother. I could see he wasn't in the mood for a chat. I just stood here in the doorway for a few minutes.'

'What was he doing?' Mitchell asked again, this time more gently.

She closed her eyes. He thought she was going to refuse to answer. 'Reading,' she said eventually. The hostility was gone now, but she seemed distant, remote from him. 'And writing', she added. 'He had sheets of paper, notebooks, journals spread out in front of him. I suppose he was preparing a lecture.'

157

'Didn't you ask him?'

She shook her head.

'Why not? You come in here, the man is one of your closest friends, you find him up to his eyeballs in paper, but you don't ask, even casually, "You look very busy, what are you doing?" '

'I said, "I didn't think you were here",' she repeated.

'You walk all the way up the stairs and down a long corridor to get here and then you say, "I didn't think you were here"?' Mitchell made it clear that his credulity was wearing thin. 'After that brilliant conversational opening, what did you talk about?

'About why neither of us was at the Burlington. I've told you all this,' she protested.

'All right. You both claimed you had to mind students. Was that the truth?'

'No, I don't think so.' Her mood changed swiftly. She sat down beside Mitchell and repeated what Peter McCormack had said the previous afternoon.

'Are you sure?'

'I'm sure that's what Peter told me. He could have been lying, but I can't see why, unless you suspect him of murdering Brian.'

'Everybody is still on the suspect list, Catherine,' he said evenly, 'particularly anybody who was in the building on Thursday night.' He hadn't meant to add the last bit — it had slipped out glibly before he could stop it — but he didn't attempt to retract it.

She blushed to the tips of her ears but said nothing.

'It's funny,' Mitchell said snidely, 'but when Maureen Brennan talked to Maeve Carty yesterday, she said something the same about you: that you had insisted that she work late on Thursday. Is Maeve making it up too?'

She looked surprised, but then gave a wry grin. 'No,

she isn't really. It depends on how you tell it, I suppose.' Without asking, she leaned across and took a cigarette out of his packet. As he lit it for her, he got the impression that she was quite relieved by the turn of question.

'Maeve is a bit of a messer.' She drew deeply on the cigarette. 'She's a nice kid but she has two left hands. We get quite a few like that — the Lord knows why they choose to do an experimental subject. Most of them get by, some of them even do quite well if they're fortunate enough to land a job where they're supervising other people and don't have to do any bench work themselves.'

She was talking too fast, too brightly. Again Mitchell suspected that she might be papering over some crack, but he said nothing and let her waffle on.

'For Maeve, disaster follows disaster. As a consequence, last week, three weeks before her report was due to be handed in, she hadn't a single experiment completed. She had another mishap last Tuesday. Not her fault this time: there was a power cut. I made her set up the experiment again on Wednesday, and it needed a solid day's work on Thursday. She was only halfway through by five o'clock, so I put my foot down and said she'd have to stay and finish it. I think she might have defied me, but Owen insisted that she stay and he volunteered to help her.' She seemed to have run out of steam but Mitchell said nothing, hoping that, in this compulsive mood, she might let slip whatever was on her mind.

'You can ask Owen about it if you don't believe me,' she said defensively, misinterpreting his silence as disbelief.

Mitchell shrugged. 'Couldn't you or Barry have looked after both students?' he asked, anxious to bring her back to the point.

'We both offered to look after the other's student, but there were no takers.'

'Did Barry give a reason?'

'He just said he was busy.'

'But you still didn't ask what he was doing?'

'I told you.' She sounded irritated, and he knew he had touched the sore point again. 'He had become so secretive that I was afraid he'd bite my head off.'

'Catherine,' Mitchell turned the chair around so that he was facing her. 'Barry was sitting here, with papers and notes all over the desk.' She nodded. 'Which ones?'

'Which what?' She sounded genuinely puzzled.

'Which papers? Which notes?' He gestured towards the desk. 'Show me which papers Barry was working on that night.'

She looked taken aback, but she leafed again through the papers on the desk. 'They're not here.'

'Sure?'

She nodded. 'There were photocopies of articles from journals, and some handwritten notes.' She tapped the papers under her hand. 'These are all typescripts.'

'So,' Mitchell said slowly, 'either Barry tidied them all away neatly before he was shot, or somebody took them.'

'Or he put them in his briefcase,' she suggested helpfully. 'Mitch!' She looked anxiously around under the desk. 'Have you got Brian's briefcase?'

He shook his head. 'Should it be here?'

'He lugged it everywhere with him. It was an enormous, battered old thing — and he crammed everything into it each evening and brought them all back again next morning.'

'The best-travelled papers in Dublin,' he said quietly, as he stood up and started poking around the room. She looked at him, startled. 'Mrs Barry told me that. It was stupid of me not to wonder what had become of it. Was it here on Thursday night?'

'Yes, it was,' she said eagerly. 'I remember now; it was open on the desk, as if Brian had just been taking things out of it. Do you think the murderer took it?'

'It certainly looks as if somebody took it.' He sat down again and put his head in his hands. 'I wish to Christ I knew what he was working on that night.'

'It was a paper.' She said it so hoarsely, it was almost a whisper.

He stared at her. 'What sort of paper?' he rasped, making no effort to disguise his anger.

'An article for a journal but I don't know what it was about. Honestly, I don't know.' Her voice was starting to break with the effort to convince him. 'I asked him but he refused to tell me.'

'Why wouldn't you tell me earlier?' His head was hurting again. 'Do you realise it's a serious offence to withhold information?'

'I wasn't "withholding" anything,' she protested. 'I just didn't think it was important. I still don't think it's important.' She was gripping the edge of the desk with both hands and staring down at them as if she'd never seen them before, avoiding Mitchell's eye.

'Let me be the judge of that,' he said ominously. 'Did he tell you what it was about?'

'No. I didn't press him. I knew from his tone that he wasn't going to tell me. He could be very stubborn — worse than me.' She grinned weakly. 'He promised I'd see it before it was published.'

'And that's all?'

'Really that's all. I'm sorry you had to drag it out of me. It didn't seem so important.' She stubbed her cigarette out in the ashtray.

He caught her wrist. 'Did you smoke a cigarette while you chatted to Barry on Thursday night?'

'Possibly.' Anxiety showed in her voice again. 'I don't remember.'

He dropped her wrist and reached into his breast

161

pocket. 'Catherine,' he said gravely as he unfolded the forensic report, 'your fingerprints are clearly identifiable on the telephone, the ashtray and the back of the spare chair. You told us you used the phone to get help, so that's all right, but how did the other prints get there?'

'I probably moved the chair to reach the phone or to feel for Brian's pulse,' she said quickly.

'There was the butt of a Carroll's in the ashtray.' Mitchell insisted. 'You're practically the only cigarette smoker in the department. So you must have been here long enough to smoke a cigarette.'

She didn't answer and they sat side by side in silence. 'We might as well eat,' Mitchell said eventually.

'I don't think I'm hungry, after all. I'll take a rain-check on lunch.' She sounded hurt and dispirited.

He hadn't the energy to discuss it. 'I'll see you tomorrow.'

'What's happening tomorrow?' Catherine asked abstractedly.

'They'll be taking the remains to the church tomorrow evening.'

'Oh God. The funeral is going to be awful, but surely you won't have to go.'

'I want to be there — for two reasons. Firstly, to pay my respects.' He turned to face her. 'Do you realise that even though I never met the man, I probably now know more about Brian Barry than about most of my friends.'

'What's the other reason?' Despite herself, she was curious.

'Oh, the usual reason that people go to funerals: to see who else is there. Barry's murderer will probably be among the mourners.'

'Oh no, Mitch. What a horrible thought! The funeral is going to be bad enough without wondering if the person beside me might be a murderer. It's not possible.'

'Of course it is.' Mitchell allowed his irritation to show again. 'Whoever killed Barry probably knew him very well. In which case he, or she, must be at the funeral. He can't possibly take the risk of his absence being noticed.'

As Mitchell was locking up, Catherine spotted a pile of bound journals on the windowsill. 'I almost forgot about the journal I wanted. Is it all right if I take it?'

'Help yourself.'

'The library will be screaming about these. It's a big concession to allow us to take journals to our offices. We're not supposed to keep them for more than three days.'

'Well you'd better take them all, so. They're not likely to be of any interest to me.'

13

Mitchell banged the door behind him as he came in, causing a draught to disturb the wall-charts on which Sam Smith was making meticulous entries from a sheaf of forms in his hand.

'There you are, sir.' Smith greeted the inspector. 'There's a whole rake of telephone messages. The Press Office has been looking for you since ten o'clock, but I said you were busy and would call them back. They wanted to issue a statement for the afternoon papers.'

Mitchell looked at his watch. 'Well, I've missed that deadline by a couple of hours. It'll be another while before they need anything for the morning papers, so we'll wait until they phone again.' He peered over Smith's shoulder. 'We haven't much to report, unless your charts can tell us anything.'

Smith stood back and inspected the charts critically. There were notes in a few of the squares but most of them were still blank. 'It's early days yet, I suppose.' He scratched his head with his pencil until the neatly combed curls sprang up again in all directions. 'We're making good progress with the interviews, but all the statements are inconclusive. Most witnesses can remember who they sat beside at the dinner, and we've been able to verify that the five members of the Genetics Department were present when the meal started, but the guests didn't sit down to dinner until ten past nine. The banqueting manager is sure he gave the waiters the nod to start serving at a quarter past. He has to worry about overtime so he was watching the clock.

'But the trouble is, sir, that none of the witnesses can produce an accurate account of their movements from group to group during the sherry reception.' Smith ran his ruler derisively across the middle of the chart, which was glaringly empty. 'The best most of them could do was to name one or two people they had spoken to during the entire hour.'

He leafed through the forms with a sigh of frustration. 'It's almost impossible to crosscheck between the witnesses. The majority of the people we've interviewed haven't been mentioned by a single one of their companions. The only one of our clients that people remember is Bob Roche. He talked to at least twenty people during the hour. The rest of those present must have spent the whole bloody evening talking to themselves.'

'It seemed such a simple idea when we discussed it.' Mitchell shared the sergeant's frustration. 'It just goes to show how singularly unmemorable most of the chat is at that sort of function. I suppose the few guests that everybody remembers were the ones who were telling funny stories or retailing the latest scandal about their colleagues.'

'Apparently, Roche is a great one for stories,' the sergeant confirmed. 'He has a stock of Kerry jokes — several people mentioned that.' He eyed the inspector warily. 'Would you like to hear a sample, sir?'

'I mightn't find it very funny.'

'Don't worry, sir. I'll tell it slowly.'

'Just for that, sergeant,' Mitchell feigned a punch at Smith's kidneys, 'you can go and make some tea.'

Mitchell perused the charts again while they waited for the kettle to boil. 'You've done a good job checking on the technical staff, Sam. They all seem accounted for.'

'Oddly enough, they were the easiest to track down, even though they were scattered all over the city.' Smith turned to admire the completed chart. 'By the way, sir, did you happen to get a chance to question Dr Morgan or Dr Gildea about their exact movements on Thursday evening?'

'Morgan claims he was in his office from six thirty. Gildea still says she talked to Barry for about a quarter of an hour at seven thirty, and thereafter she was in her room. However, I'm not happy about her evidence.' He explained to the sergeant about the missing briefcase and Catherine Gildea's less than satisfactory response to the forensic report.

'Anyway, it won't help your charts, Sam. Both Morgan and Gildea claim they were sitting reading in their respective rooms at the material time. There's no corroborative evidence.'

'It's a funny life, isn't it sir?' The sergeant put two mugs of tea on the desk and sat down opposite Mitchell. 'Spending the whole evening locked away reading books. They must be very knowledgeable altogether.'

'What use is it?' Mitchell asked ungraciously. 'You know what they say about academics, Sam. They get to know more and more about less and less, until eventually they know everything about nothing.'

'Still and all, it must be great,' Smith sounded wistful. 'When I was at the Brothers I used to dream about going to university, maybe doing languages and being able to read books in French or German — but', he sighed philosophically, 'I didn't get good enough marks in the Leaving

166

to qualify for a scholarship.'

'You could do a degree at night, Sam,' Mitchell surprised himself by suggesting.

'Ah, it's a bit late in the day now to be going back to studying, sir.' He seemed anxious to dismiss the idea. 'Besides, I haven't got that many free evenings. When I'm not on duty there's this youth club in Finglas where I do a bit of work. I wouldn't want to let the kids down.'

'If you really want to do it, Sam, you'll find time for it.' Mitchell didn't feel like prolonging the discussion, and got up from the desk to stare at the charts again.

'Most of the undergraduates are accounted for too, sir.' Smith, glad of Mitchell's decision to change the subject, looked over the inspector's shoulder. 'A group of them were together in the library, and most of the rest were at home or with friends.'

'That reminds me. I need to see young McCormack again.'

*　*　*

McCormack looked sulky when he walked in half an hour later. 'My dad says I should have a solicitor if you're going to go on questioning me like this,' he announced belligerently.

'Peter, sit here like a good lad and I'll get you a cup of tea.' Smith cleared some space at the desk and moved up a chair for the student. 'The inspector just wants to talk to you. There's no call to bite his head off.' He spoke firmly and, to Mitchell's surprise, McCormack submitted without demur.

'Peter, I'd like you to go through your statement with us again. You realise that, as one of the few people in the building when Professor Barry was shot, you are a key witness in the case,' Mitchell shamelessly resorted to flattery, 'so your evidence is very important.'

167

He read the first few lines of the statement aloud. ' "I was working in the O'Meara Building on the night of the sixth of March, because I had to finish an important experiment for my research project." Now, Peter, have we got that accurately?'

The young man nodded, but without conviction.

'Peter, wouldn't it be fairer to say that you were working in the lab because Professor Barry said he'd be there and suggested that it would be an opportunity for you to work late?'

'I suppose so, but I don't see the difference.'

'It might not have made much difference to you, but it's important to us to know that the professor planned to stay in the lab. It wasn't just something that he found he had to do at the last minute.'

'No. On his way to coffee he told me that he'd be there late,' McCormack agreed.

Mitchell looked at the statement again. 'You went to tea at six o'clock and came back to the lab about seven, is that right?'

McCormack nodded.

'Did you see Professor Barry at that stage?'

'Only for a minute. I was just back in the lab when he stuck his head out of the office to ask me what time I'd be finished. I told him that I had to use Dr Lalor's centrifuge in the other wing, but that I'd have everything done by nine o'clock. He said I was to let him know when I was going home, but not to disturb him in the meantime.'

'What time did you go over to the other wing?'

'About a quarter past seven.'

'And you were still over there when Dr Gildea and Owen O'Neill came to tell you about Professor Barry's death?'

'That's right.'

'You didn't come back to Professor Barry's lab at all?'

168

'No.' McCormack shook his head vigorously, but said, as an afterthought, 'Except to get a spare tube, but that only took me a few minutes.'

'Let's have that again, Peter.'

'I was in the other wing all the time, except for the few minutes it took to come back to my own bench to collect a spare centrifuge tube. One of the tubes I'd brought with me was cracked, and I was afraid it would leak in the centrifuge, so I came back to the lab to get another one.'

'Did you see Barry, or anybody else, when you came back?'

'No, he was in his office.'

'Are you sure?'

'Yes, he was talking to Katy — Dr Gildea, I mean.'

'Did you see Dr Gildea?'

'No, I just heard them yelling at each other.'

'Yelling?'

'They were having an argument. Both their voices were raised.'

'Why didn't you mention any of this in your original statement, Peter?' Mitchell tried not to show his irritation.

'Nobody asked me, and I suppose I forgot about it myself.'

'Was it so unremarkable for two members of staff to be having a row that you wouldn't remember it?' Mitchell leaned back in his chair and regarded the student sceptically.

'It wasn't unusual,' Peter insisted. ' Katy and the prof were good friends. They often had rows.'

'What about?'

'All sorts of things. They were always arguing about selection.'

'Selection?' Mitchell was at a loss.

'Natural selection. The prof was a great Darwinist and he and Katy used to have heated arguments about evolution,' he explained enthusiastically. 'We used all join in.'

'And you think this was just another academic argument?'

'I don't know. I couldn't really hear what they were saying, but Katy sounded quite cross. I heard her say something like, "I did all the work." I think they were discussing some paper they were drafting, but I was only in the room for two minutes so I don't really know.'

'What time was this, Peter?'

'About eight o'clock.'

*   *   *

The library was oppressively silent when Catherine Gildea elbowed her way through the swing doors, carrying the journals from Brian Barry's office. The students, realising that their examinations were only ten weeks away, were desperately making up for lost time.

She had sat in her office for a while after lunch, trying unsuccessfully to concentrate on the thesis of the unfortunate young man whose results had gone up in flames, but she decided that her attention was too distracted and that it would be quite unfair, in her state of mind, to attempt to assess his work. Noticing the journals she had rescued from Brian Barry's office, she was glad to find an excuse to walk across the campus to the library. By the time she got there, her arms were aching and she dumped the journals unceremoniously on the issue desk.

The assistant's reaction to her explanation for the overdue return of the journals suggested to Catherine that death was an inadequate excuse for breaching library regulations.

Catherine picked up one of the volumes from the desk.

'Dr Gildea, please make up your mind whether or not you are returning these volumes. You're the first to complain when something is missing!'

'I'm sorry, Roisin, I want to photocopy an article.' She lacked the energy for an argument.

'I'll leave these volumes here. Be sure to put that one back with the others.'

As she waited for the photocopier, Catherine glanced down the contents page, looking for the article she needed.

When she had finished her photocopying, she returned the journal to the issue desk and started to scan the lists of articles in the other volumes.

'Dr Gildea, are you finished with those journals?'

'I'm sorry, Roisin. I was just looking for something, but I've found it now. Thank you.'

14

The brief prayers that marked the arrival of Brian Barry's mortal remains at the church were just ending as Mitchell arrived. He found a vantage point where the concrete forecourt sloped upward towards some shrubs. From here he watched the mourners emerge from the church.

The crowd was enormous. A man like Barry would have had a numerous aquaintance, but, Mitchell suspected, friends and colleagues were augmented by the merely curious, attracted by the publicity surrounding the murder. Anna Barry, supported by her fifteen-year-old son and followed closely by her mother-in-law with the younger children, was making her way slowly towards the waiting car. Mitchell admired her composure as she shook hands and acknowledged expressions of sympathy from friends and acquaintances who pressed around her.

Mitchell disliked funerals and usually dodged the ritual expression of condolences to the bereaved. As he watched Anna Barry, he recalled the day his father had been buried from the little chapel beside the schoolhouse where he had taught for thirty-nine years. The crowd had converged on the family, and he had wanted to escape, but when all the past pupils of the little school, his sister's pals from the convent and his own classmates from Templemore, not to mention first and second cousins from all over the country, had shaken him warmly by the hand, the panic had subsided and he had found himself chatting to them about his father. At first it hadn't been easy, but soon he was enjoying it, hearing stories about the old man that he'd never heard before. When the condolences had started, he remembered hoping that at last he might discover the correct form of words for such occasions, but afterwards he couldn't remember a single word except for a few outrageous stories that some of the old men had told about his father, which wouldn't be of any help to him at all in the future.

Now, he wondered what any of the people around Anna Barry could find to say that might be of comfort to her. It was one thing to utter routine words of sympathy on the passing of an elderly schoolmaster, who had died peacefully in his bed after three score years and ten, but what could you say to the widow of a comparatively young man, whose successful academic career had been cut short by cold-blooded murder?

Mitchell recognised many of the faces in the crowd. All the staff of the Genetics Department were there. They stood in a group with the postgraduate and fourth-year students. Mitchell identified the vice-chancellor, a distinguished bearded man who was talking to Anna, both his hands paternally clasping hers.

Other faces in the crowd were vaguely familiar: a couple of deputies from the oppositon benches, present, presumably, because of Anna Barry's membership of their party; a High Court judge and a brace of solicitors whom Mitchell recognised from his appearances in court; Michael McDevitt, standing with his back to the Barrys, engrossed in earnest converstion with a journalist from

The Irish Times.

The Dublin middle class burying its dead was as much a ritual as any bunch of painted savages that you'd see in a documentary film, Mitchell decided. As if echoing his thoughts, he overheard a man behind him remark, 'The university may not treat us too well when we're alive but they certainly do a great funeral.'

Out of the corner of his eye Mitchell spotted Jim Gannon standing alone on the edge of the group around Anna Barry. He took advantage of the ebb and flow of sympathisers to drift unobtrusively towards him.

'I was expecting a call from you,' Gannon mouthed as Mitchell reached his side.

'I rang your office a couple of times but I didn't want to provoke your secretary's curiosity by leaving my name.' Mitchell murmured. 'I had a quiet word with Paddy Lynch last night. He's prepared to give us a statement, if we need one, that Mrs B was on the premises at the material time. I'll keep your name out of the file if I can, but I know where to catch up with you if I have to.'

'Thanks, Mitch.' Gannon grasped the inspector's arm warmly. 'I appreciate that — as much for Anna's sake as for myself. I wish to Christ', he said emotionally, 'that I could go and talk to her now, but I'm afraid of embarrassing her, particularly in front of her mother-in-law.'

The two men turned to watch Anna Barry. 'Will you look at those bastards!' Gannon involuntarily took a step forward towards the Barrys as a couple of press photographers elbowed their way through the crowd for a close-up of Anna talking to sympathisers.

Mitchell laid a restraining hand on Gannon's arm before impelling himself through the crowd as politely as he could.

'All right, lads.' He flashed his identification card at one of the press men. 'Have a bit of respect now and leave

174

the family in peace.'

One of the photographers muttered something under his breath, but he and his colleague withdrew peaceably enough to take pictures of some of the notables in the crowd.

After the family had left in the large black funeral cars, the mourners gradually dispersed; knots of people drifting off towards the car park. Mitchell made his way through the thinning crowd towards the church. To atone for his absence from the prayers for the dead, he slipped in through the swing doors and stood for a few minutes in the shadows under the organ loft, savouring the smells of incense and beeswax as the clerk extinguished the candles that stood beside the coffin. It struck him as strange that the remains of the deceased should be so casually abandoned after the short ceremony and be left to a lonely vigil in the empty church. His thoughts about death were interrupted by the sound of footsteps, and he turned to find Catherine Gildea standing beside him.

'Anna asked me to look for you,' she said, as if feeling that some explanation of her presence was required. 'She wanted to thank you for rescuing her from the press. A few of Brian's close friends have been asked back to the house for a drink. Anna said I was to invite you, but I can make your apologies if you'd rather not come.'

'It's very kind of Mrs Barry. I'll certainly come.'

He was distinctly aware that Catherine Gildea was not pleased by his alacrity in accepting the invitation and was surprised that she agreed to his offer of a lift. To break the awkward silence that settled between them in the car, he ventured, 'Isn't it a bit odd that an Englishwoman like Mrs Barry should be bringing people back to the house on a night like this? That's surely one of our customs that the English find hardest to understand.'

'Oh, I think Anna is a classic case of the English who become more Irish than ourselves,' Catherine Gildea said absently. She lapsed into silence again and played with her gloves, stretching the leather between her hands. 'It has a certain compulsive logic. For me, the alternative would be going home to an empty house to weep into a bottle of whiskey. Communal grieving may be a bit macabre, but it beats hell out of that.'

* * *

The sittingroom of the Barrys' house was already full, and any silencing effect of grief was being dispelled by the glasses of whiskey and sherry that the older children were being handed around. As Mitchell followed Catherine Gildea into the room, she was flamboyantly greeted by a man whose right leg was encased in plaster.

'Whatever happened to your poor leg, Sean?' Mitchell heard her enquire. Presumably the alcoholic brother, he surmised and ostentatiously stepped out of earshot to almost collide with Chris O'Mahony, who was standing in a corner surveying the gathering with a jaundiced eye.

'Still on duty, inspector, or can I get you a drink?' Without waiting for an answer, he secured whiskeys for both of them.

'So we can bury poor old Brian in sanctified ground tomorrow.' O'Mahony raised his glass to the inspector. 'The papers say you now definitely suspect foul play.'

'I believe the church takes a more forgiving view of suicide these days, Dr O'Mahony.' Mitchell sidestepped the issue.

'But you think it was murder?' O'Mahony wasn't to be so easily put off.

'That's for the coroner to decide.'

'I don't believe you'd be here this evening if you weren't keeping an eye on us as murder suspects.'

176

'Very well, Dr O'Mahony.' Mitchell lost his patience. 'If you insist that I should be working, perhaps you'd tell me where you were last Thursday between eight and nine o'clock, when you were supposed to be at the Institute's sherry reception?'

'You have been doing your homework, inspector.' O'Mahony looked impressed but not unduly disturbed. 'I was in the bar of the Burlington having a couple of quiet pints. Sherry isn't my tipple, and that crowd of pompous academics saying "rhubarb, rhubarb, rhubarb" isn't my scene.'

'You were on your own in the bar?'

'Yes, but the barman should remember me. I unburdened myself to him on the subject of Conor's lecture.'

'You were there all the time between the lecture and the dinner?'

'Yes, I needed several pints to recover from that boring old —' O'Mahony broke off in mid-sentence and blushed to the roots of his fair hair. 'Hello there, Conor; enjoying the party?' Realising that this was hardly appropriate, he blushed a deeper crimson and coughed to dissipate his embarrassment.

'Professor,' Mitchell turned to greet Conor Dodd, wondering how long he had been standing within earshot. 'Dr O'Mahony has been telling me how much he enjoyed your lecture on Thursday.' O'Mahony, who had just taken a large mouthful of whiskey in an effort to regain his composure, was overcome by another fit of coughing and withdrew, ostensibly to find a glass of water.

'Funny lad,' Dodd said equivocally as he gazed at his retreating colleague. 'You're making progress with your enquiries, I trust, inspector? Or perhaps I shouldn't ask?'

'Oh, these investigations are always slow and painstaking,' Mitchell said automatically but, bored by the usual clichés, added, 'It's a bit like scientific research, professor. A fact here, a suspicion there — it's only when you put it all together that you finally have a theory. And then you have to test your theory. It can't be rushed.'

Dodd looked a little startled by the analogy, but said unemotionally, 'Well, all Brian's colleagues will be relieved to see a successful outcome to your investigation, inspector, though we must pray that nothing will emerge to damage the reputation of the department.'

'I hope not.'

In the ensuing thoughtful pause, Mitchell became aware of Sean Barry's proximity again.

'It was a secret mission, *a stóir*. Sure amn't I lucky to be here at all.' Sean Barry dropped his voice to a dramatic whisper, audible to Mitchell, if not to the entire room. 'But I have to be careful what I say in front of your man.' He winked at Catherine Gildea and indicated Mitchell with a sideways nod of his head. 'Not that you can tell, of course, he wouldn't be the first peeler to be quietly on our side.'

Despite his plastercast, Barry executed a nimble hop that brought him face to face with Mitchell, who had been trying studiously to ignore him. 'Mightn't that be so?' he asked the inspector. Receiving no reply, he persisted, 'Indeed it might, and you the son of old Batty Mitchell. Ah, that was the time when Irishmen would stand up and be counted — not like that renegade brother of mine, God be good to him. The things he used to be writing in that shoneen newspaper. But what could you expect, what with him married to a Brit and all? Not but that she's a decent woman in her own way,' he added magnanimously, as he took a large swallow of Anna Barry's whiskey and looked around hopefully for somebody to replenish his glass.

Taking advantage of this distraction, Mitchell excused himself from Conor Dodd and went to talk to his hostess, who had just entered the room. In reply to her thanks for his attendance at the funeral and his intervention with the press, he found himself talking to her frankly and naturally about her late husband. As he did so, he began to understand why Anna Barry had invited so many of the mourners to be with her this night. She simply wanted to be with people who would talk to her about Brian.

When their tête-à-tête was interrupted by the arrival of more guests, Anna Barry said to him quietly, 'I think Catherine looks very tired and strained. I noticed her slipping out of the room a while ago, probably to escape from poor Sean, but I haven't seen her come back. Could you see if she's all right?'

There was no sign of her in the hall, so Mitchell looked into the kitchen, where a woman in a flowered apron was buttering slices of bread.

'Have you seen Dr Gildea?' he asked her.

'No, she's not here, sir. She probably went upstairs. She might be in the bathroom or in Mrs Barry's bedroom.'

Feeling suddenly anxious, Mitchell ran lightly up the thickly carpeted stairs. Five doors led off the landing. The door facing him, which was ajar, led into an empty bathroom. He tried the next door and was surprised to find it locked, until he remembered that it was the door to the study, which he had locked himself on Sunday. The light was on in the bedroom next door, but when he went in there was no sign of anybody. Thinking that Gildea might be in the bathroom leading off the bedroom, he tried the door. It wasn't locked and he opened it cautiously. The bathroom was empty, but the door in the opposite wall, which connected it to the study, was open and through it he could see her, standing with her back to him, searching systematically through the drawers of the desk. With a sense of shock, Mitchell stood for a moment watching her. Despite his growing doubts about the truthfulness of her statements, he hadn't yet brought himself to believe that she was implicated in Barry's death.

As he walked through the bathrom into the study, things started to fall into place in his mind and he felt a slow anger at his own gullibility. 'May I ask what you are doing, Catherine, and, for that matter, how you got in here?'

'That must be perfectly obvious since you've just come through the same door yourself.' She looked up from her search, a bunch of manilla folders in her hand. She sounded irritable but not alarmed.

The calmness of her reply infuriated him. 'All right, I slipped up by not locking this door,' he admitted. 'However, since you're obviously engaged in a thorough search of that desk, don't expect me to believe that you strayed in here out of idle curiosity.'

'No, Mitch, I'm looking for the missing notebooks.' She looked him squarely in the face. 'But they're not here.'

'How did you manage to open the desk? I'm certain it was locked when I was here on Sunday.'

'I told you I had duplicates of all Brian's keys, including the key of this desk, and — '

'And you brought the key with you so that you could search the desk,' he pre-empted her explanation. 'No wonder you didn't want me to come.' He strode across the room and took the files from her hand. 'Why didn't you ask me to open it for you?'

'Why are you so angry? I didn't come here intending to look for the notebooks. I came upstairs to get away from Seán. At the best of times he and his like make me want to throw up. Tonight he literally made me feel ill. There was somebody in the main bathroom, so I used Anna's bathroom. I knew she wouldn't mind — we always use it when there's a party in the house. Sheer curiosity made me unbolt the door into the study. I was surprised to find it unlocked.' She seemed intimidated by Mitchell's nearness, and moved away from the desk and flopped into the armchair. 'It was only when I saw the desk that I thought the notebooks might be in it, and remembered I had the spare key in my handbag. For God's sake, Mitch, I wasn't even being secretive about it.' Her eyes pleaded with him to believe her, but he refused to respond. 'If I didn't want to be seen I'd have bolted the bathroom door on this side.'

'Really, Catherine, for somebody who has the reputation of being very clever you're behaving extremely stupidly. By rights I should —'

What Mitchell ought to have done under the circumstances was never revealed because their confrontation was interrupted by Anna Barry, who poked her head through the bathroom door.

'Is something wrong? Catherine, are you feeling all right? You look very pale.'

'Anna, I'm really sorry.' Catherine Gildea jumped to her feet. 'Inspector Mitchell caught me red-handed going through Brian's desk looking for some notebooks that are missing from the lab. The inspector is cross because he thinks I should have asked his permission. I'm very embarrassed because I realise that I should have asked yours. I do apologise.'

'My dear,' Anna looked her in the eye, 'I think you and I have always understood each other. Brian kept nothing in that desk except papers related to his work, so as far as I'm concerned you are welcome to open it if you need something.' She turned to Mitchell. 'Now, inspector, do stop playing silly buggers and help Catherine to find whatever it is she's looking for and then both of you come downstairs. Mrs O'Daly has made sandwiches and I'd better go down and start handing them around.'

Mitchell maintained a stubborn silence as he bundled

papers and files back into the desk and locked it with Catherine Gildea's keys, which he pocketed, saying tersely, 'It's probably better if I take care of these for the moment.'

He followed Catherine Gildea down the stairs. When she reached the hall, a group of her colleagues greeted her with derisive remarks.

'I hear the copper caught you with your hand in the till, Cath,' Chris O'Mahony teased her.

Anna Barry, who was standing at the bottom of the stairs holding a plate of sandwiches, felt constrained to apologise. 'I'm sorry. I shouldn't have said anything, but it seemed so ironic that poor Inspector Mitchell should be upset because you were looking through those awful old papers that I was always trying to persuade Brian to throw out. I couldn't resist telling Bob and the others about it.'

'What on earth were you doing, Catherine?' Conor Dodd looked up from inspecting the sandwiches.

'Trying to recover incriminating evidence before the police could find it,' chimed in O'Mahony.

Mitchell, distinctly unamused at finding the incident turned into a departmental joke, was nevertheless surprised by Catherine's sharpness as she turned on her tormentor. 'Chris, you never cease to amaze me with your unfailing bad taste. As a matter of fact I was looking for some notebooks that seem to have disappeared from Brian's lab.' She turned her back contemptuously on O'Mahony, and vented her spleen on Mitchell. 'However, I don't think the inspector believes me.'

O'Mahony, obviously suffering from the effects of drinking on an empty stomach, was stung by her tone. 'Inspector, you must believe our Cath. She's a senior lecturer, you know. They're very trustworthy people. You're meant to be a detective. Why don't you find the lady's notebooks for her?'

'Don't worry, Dr O'Mahony,' Mitchell snapped, 'I'll find those bloody notebooks tomorrow if I have to take the whole O'Meara Building apart.'

Gildea ignored the exchange and turned on her heel. 'I'll just say good night to Brian's mother. I'd be grateful if you would drive me home, inspector. Then Chris can entertain the others with jokes about my leaving in police custody.'

15

Mitchell turned the car sharply in the street outside Catherine Gildea's house, and headed towards the shore. He parked on Strand Road, pulled on the rubber boots he kept in the back of the car, and set out across the wet strand. It was quite dark by now, but it was a clear night and the street lights cast a pink glow over the city. Only a handful of dog-walkers and lugworm-hunters remained on the beach.

It was several years since he had walked on Sandymount Strand. When he had first been posted to Dublin, almost twenty years ago, he had felt stifled by the concrete wilderness of the city and homesick for the open coastline of the west of Ireland. His chance renting of a flat near the strand had been an important factor in his adaptation to urban life. Depressed at first by the houses and apartment blocks that flanked the beach and the landscape of power stations and gantrys, he had gradually learned to enjoy its utilitarian beauty. His first summer in Dublin, he'd been mostly on night duty and had often come here at the end of the shift to watch the sun rise over Howth Head. He would always remember how the silver-painted fuel tanks in the port caught the first rays of light minutes before the sun itself appeared over the horizon to set the sea on fire and turn the windows of the sleeping houses to molten gold.

In those days he had used the strand as an antidote to the sordid side of his job. As he became more senior in the force, he took long, damp walks along the shoreline to think through difficult cases, but for some years past he had come here less often.

Tonight he walked quickly, his mind racing, but the old magic worked: the cold sea air gradually calmed him; his pace became more relaxed and his thoughts more ordered.

From the beginning, circumstantial evidence had placed Catherine Gildea high on his list of suspects. The disingenuous behaviour he had witnessed tonight further incriminated her. He finally realised that his feelings for her were of no account. From now on, she was the prime suspect.

He picked up a piece of rock and threw it far into the distance. There was an angry squawk, and an oyster-catcher took off over his head. He wanted to retort and shout his frustration at the bird, but the habits of years of discipline restrained him. It was just his bloody luck: the first time in a decade that he had felt something for a woman and she turned out to be a murderer!

The argument that it was Catherine who had cautioned against their developing relationship brought him no comfort. Whatever else she might be, Catherine was undeniably a very clever woman. In effect she had seduced him. He could see that now: she had filled him with whiskey, aroused him with the story of her love affair with Brian Barry and then let nature take its course. Her subsequent ploy of holding him at arm's length had been simply a strategy to maintain his interest.

He could, of course, ask O'Loughlin to take him off

the case without admitting the extent of his emotional entanglement. The old man had already sniffed out his growing interest in Catherine Gildea, and would probably choose to avoid embarrassment by asking no awkward questions. It would be the sensible thing to do, he told himself, but every instinct rejected that course of action. He had never asked to be relieved of a case; his objectivity had never come into question. He was damned if he would allow any woman to come between him and his job.

Engrossed in these recriminations, he found he had reached the incoming tide. The water was lapping round his ankles when he turned to retrace his steps towards his car. The lights from the houses along Strand Road shone warmly across the beach. The tranquillity of the night was balm to his damaged self-respect, and he began to accept the truth. He had been a credulous fool. He recognised that now and started to rationalise his position. If Catherine's feelings for him were insincere, then he had sustained no loss, was no worse off than before he met her. The formula was almost successful.

The whole bloody mess must be disposed of as quickly as possible. Having reached this decision, he felt his ideas crystallise. What he needed now was hard, factual evidence. He had spent too much time talking, hoping to unravel the complex relationships between the victim and those closest to him, but he would make no progress without evidence of motive and must concentrate on finding that. Everything pointed to the existence, somewhere, of an incriminating document. The signs of interference with Barry's box of correspondence, the missing briefcase, Catherine's request for access to his office, and now her clandestine search of the study — all suggested that some important piece of evidence was still at large.

Mitchell felt almost cheerful when he stopped at the garda station in Irishtown to phone O'Loughlin. The superintendent sounded pleased by Mitchell's request to see him and suggested that they should meet in his local pub.

* * *

O'Loughlin was halfway through his first pint by the time Mitchell joined him in the lounge of The Bottle Tower. He raised an eyebrow when the younger man ordered a large whiskey for himself as well as a fresh pint for O'Loughlin.

'Is there something to celebrate? Have we got our man for the Barry murder?'

'No, but there's a woman with a lot of questions to answer.' Mitchell wished the superintendent health and took a large mouthful of neat whiskey. 'I'd like to bring Catherine Gildea in for further questioning.'

'What's the case against her?'

'Very straightforward, sir. She had means and opportunity. There's no question about that. Everybody else has some sort of alibi, even if the alibi for those at the Burlington isn't perfect.'

'Motive?'

'She had a row with Barry less than an hour before he died. I'm certain there's something she's not telling us. Her account of that last conversation with Barry is very confused, and she keeps contradicting herself. Then I caught her raiding Barry's desk.' He explained what had happened. 'She claimed she was looking for some notebooks.'

'It's a perfectly credible explanation.' O'Loughlin seemed determined to be obstructive.

'I can't accept it, sir.' Mitchell was finding his superior's scepticism exasperating. 'If that was all she wanted, she had only to ask me to open the desk for her. We spent half yesterday hunting for those wretched notebooks in Barry's office. She knew I was willing to help her.' He realised he sounded petulant and tried to disguise his resentment. 'Yesterday I pointed out to her bluntly how vulnerable her situation was, and I think she panicked and took the risk of searching Barry's desk when the chance came her way this evening.'

'What do you think she was looking for?'

'I don't know, sir. My hunch is that there's a document, possibly a letter, that would reveal her motive for wanting Barry out of the way.'

'What are you proposing to do?' O'Loughlin was still not convinced.

'I'd like to bring her in for questioning, find out what she was looking for.'

'You've interviewed her several times already.'

Mitchell nodded. 'You could say she's been very co-operative.' He picked up a beer-mat and examined it closely. 'She's a clever woman. She has a knack of appearing open and frank, but she tells only what she wants you to know and no more. That's why I want you to question her, sir. I think if we bring her into the station, between us we might get nearer the truth.'

Mitchell tore the beer-mat into little fragments while O'Loughlin puffed calmly at his pipe and considered the suggestion.

'You've got damn all evidence, Mitch. There's no motive except Gildea's own admission that she had an affair with Barry years ago. That hardly constitutes a reason for murder.'

'She had a row with Barry less than an hour before he was shot, sir.' Mitchell was not prepared to give in without an argument.

'You're not looking objectively at this case.' To forestall

any objections, O'Loughlin summoned the barman and ordered two whiskeys. When they arrived he made a great performance of counting out the exact change. After he had completed this transaction, he sat back and sipped the whiskey appreciatively.

'There are two reasons why I don't want you to make a complete ass of yourself, Mitch. Firstly, you're a bright lad with a promising career ahead of you, if you mind your step. Secondly, and more importantly, if you get your head covered in shit, some of it is bound to fall on me.' He looked across the table at Mitchell to see how he was reacting, but the inspector was engrossed in the destruction of another beer-mat. 'Last Saturday, I considered taking you off the case, because I thought you were letting that wee girl pull the wool over your eyes. I needn't have worried; I should know you better by now. I suspect the worst crime the woman has committed is to have succumbed to your charm and, in your book, that must betray an ulterior motive.'

'That's not fair, sir. I admit I found the woman attractive — any man would — but I have been careful not to let that influence my judgement.'

'All right, lad.' O'Loughlin held up a hand to silence the inspector's protestations. 'As a test of your objectivity, let's talk about other suspects: Gildea's colleagues, for instance.'

Mitchell, with mixed feelings about the turn the discussion was taking, counted off the staff of the Genetics Department on his fingers. 'Starting at the top, Bob Roche certainly had the means—there's no corroborative evidence that his gun was stolen. His only obvious motive is resentment about Barry's role in the contest for the chair, but that was fifteen years ago. Why should that old feud surface again now? Anyway, he's the one person that several witnesses remember talking to at the hotel between eight and nine o'clock.

'Like everybody else on the staff, Conor Dodd had access to the gun; he was at the party where we think it was stolen. However, we've found no motive, and he had only limited opportunity. After all, he was giving a lecture on the night of the murder.

'Chris O'Mahony is a more attractive candidate. He was at Roche's party and certainly knew where the gun was kept. He's obviously bitter about Barry's part in stopping his promotion and he strikes me as being quite unbalanced. He could have slipped away unnoticed from the Burlington. He skipped the reception, but claims the barman can confirm that he was in the bar. Tonight's the barman's night off, but Sam is tracking him down to check O'Mahony's story.

'Paul Mooney and Colette Lalor were together all evening, and Bob Roche seems to have gone to some trouble to introduce them to his friends. Several witnesses remember meeting them at the reception. While Morgan had as much opportunity as Gildea, he was never in Roche's house and nobody can suggest a motive unless he's a member of some mournful Welsh druidic society that sacrifices professors at the full moon.'

Mitchell paused to light a cigarette. The superintendent eyed him thoughtfully. 'What about your man that's away?'

'Gerry Flynn? I haven't succeeded in contacting him, but the Swiss border police say he crossed into Austria on the morning of the seventh — that's last Friday.'

'I meant the other fellow, the one who's in Canada.'

'I've had a fax from the RCMP confirming that Pat McIvor hasn't left Vancouver. The only other suspect on my list is the student, McCormack. He had opportunity, and a motive of sorts, but it would have been difficult for him to get hold of Roche's gun.'

'Anybody else — friends, relatives? What about Mrs Barry and her mysterious whereabouts on Thursday evening?'

O'Loughlin raised an eyebrow when Mitchell repeated Anna Barry's story, but the inspector assured him, 'They're both in the clear. The publican will swear that she and Gannon came in together no later than eight thirty.

'Sean Barry has an alibi too. The Branch checked him for us. His war wound was acquired falling off a bar stool in Davy Byrne's on Thursday afternoon. At eight thirty he was in the casualty unit in Vincent's having a plaster cast put on his leg.'

'You need a lot more evidence before we can think of charging anyone.' O'Loughlin knocked back the last of his whiskey and looked pointedly at his empty glass.

'Let's pursue your theory of a missing document.' O'Loughlin had obviously decided to adopt a more constuctive attitude while Mitchell was ordering the drinks. 'Has that building been thoroughly searched?'

'We took a good look through it the day after the murder but, sure, we didn't know what it was we were looking for then, sir.'

'Why not search the entire building again and see if you can find Barry's briefcase or any other evidence? You might even find Dr Gildea's notebooks.'

'I'll take the place apart, sir, but I'm willing to bet we won't find those notebooks. I don't believe they exist.'

'Hasn't it occurred to you at all, Mitch,' O'Loughlin burrowed in his pockets for his tobacco pouch, 'that those notebooks could be the incriminating evidence you're looking for?'

'They're only students' workbooks, sir. They wouldn't be of any interest to us.'

'Well, isn't that what this case is all about — work?'

O'Loughlin leaned forward with uncharacteristic enthusiasm. 'Barry is killed in his laboratory, papers are missing, his briefcase is stolen; even the gun belongs to another scientist. Science is very competitive today.' He emphasised his point by wagging the stem of his pipe at Mitchell. 'Read the business pages of the paper any day; there's big money in this biotechnology, and scientific reputations are made and lost overnight.

'Maybe Gildea had a motive,' O'Loughlin continued pensively as he began excavating the bowl of his pipe with a nail-file. 'There's a row between Barry and Gildea just before he's killed. You're sceptical because she claims they were only discussing their research, and you want to think it was about sex. Maybe she's telling the truth, Mitch, and the argument *was* about her work, but the subject was so inflammatory that she killed Barry because of it.' He looked triumphantly at the inspector. 'And the evidence is in those notebooks.'

Mitchell refused to comment on the theory. 'I'll have the O'Meara building searched from top to bottom tomorrow. Fortunately, it's officially closed all day because of the funeral, so we won't have problems with the authorities. I'll also personally search Barry's house, if Mrs Barry has no objection.'

Deciding on a course of action had invigorated Mitchell and he stood up purposefully, scattering shreds of beer mat on the carpet. 'If we draw a blank, then I suggest we need search warrants for the homes of the other members of staff, including Gildea.'

'Right.' O'Loughlin knocked back the dregs in his glass and got slowly to his feet. 'Whatever your personal feelings, Mitch, promise me one thing. I want you making no move against this woman until you clear it with me first.'

16

'Catherine! Come in.'

'Jacky, I'm sorry to call so late but I'm frantic about those notebooks. I can't find them anywhere — are you sure Gerry couldn't have left them here.'

Jacky Whelan dropped the chain off the front door. 'Come in. It isn't late at all. Actually, I've only just come in myself,' she said nonchalantly, 'I went back to the lab after being at the church.'

Catherine Gildea refrained from comment as she followed the student up the narrow stairs to the first floor. The flat was over a chemist's shop, and a faintly medicinal odour permeated the building.

'Do you have to find Gerry's notebook tonight?' Jacky led the way into the kitchen. It was a large, high-ceilinged room. The scrubbed deal table that occupied most of the space apparently served as dining table, dressing table, and desk, and was covered with an extensive collection of objects, from books to cosmetics, all interspersed with dirty china and glasses. Jacky made no effort to disguise or apologise for the confusion. She deftly redistributed some of the clutter to clear a space at one end of the table and rescued two pottery mugs, which she rinsed out and dried with a surprisingly clean tea-towel.

'Wouldn't the prof give Peter an extension on the deadline for handing in his report?' Jacky, without consulting her guest, had made coffee. 'His circumstances are exceptional.'

'He probably will. I haven't asked him.' Catherine took the mug of coffee Jacky handed to her and abstractedly added milk from a cardboard carton. The liquid came out too fast, filling the mug to the rim. 'I have to know what Gerry was doing after Christmas.' She stared at Jacky through the steam rising from the coffee. 'I've got to find out as soon as possible. You're sure you don't know anything more than you've told me?'

Jacky shook her head, awed by the hint of panic in the older woman's demeanour 'I only know that he was measuring RNA and cAMP. I didn't see more than a page or two of his results.'

'Why did you think he was repeating Peter's work?'

'Gerry let slip something about "having to reproduce exactly the same conditions", one time I asked him why he was using the old centrifuge downstairs instead of the new one in our lab. He wasn't very good at being secretive.'

'But he could have been repeating anybody's work, he didn't specifically mention Peter, did he?'

Jacky brushed the objection aside. 'It had to be Peter's, because he was measuring cAMP.'

'Is there any chance that Gerry might have kept copies of his results? Wasn't he a student in Cork when they had that fire in the labs?'

'Yes, he was.' Jacky's mug of coffee remained suspended in mid-air. 'He was having his thesis typed when it happened, otherwise he'd have lost all his data. He's so horribly sensible that I wouldn't be surprised if he keeps copies of everything now.' She put down the mug and stood up excitedly. 'He left a suitcase full of papers in the bedroom. Let's take a look at that.'

'I don't like to ask you to interfere with Gerry's private papers,' Gildea protested, without conviction.

Jacky was already on her way into the bedroom. She grinned sardonically as she knelt to pull a battered suitcase from under the bed. 'You needn't worry. He must know I'd inspect the contents if he left it here. I had a glance through it the night after he went away, as a matter of fact, but it all seemed terribly dull.' She opened the case and piles of loose sheets spilled out on the carpet. Picking up an armful of them, she thrust them at Catherine, who showed no scruples in examining them page by page. After twenty minutes the bed and the floor were littered with paper. The two women looked at each other in disappointment. 'These are only drafts of his thesis and some old lecture notes.' Gildea sounded weary and dispirited.

'I've never seen such a load of junk.' Jacky was so disgusted that she kicked the empty suitcase back under the bed and, abandoning the mess, went back to the kitchen.

'What's the point of keeping all that?' She addressed the question to a photograph of the absent Gerry that was stuck in the corner of a mirror in the hall.

Catherine looked forlornly at the papers on the bed and made an ineffectual effort to gather them back into some kind of order, but she lacked the energy to complete the task. She shrugged her shoulders and followed Jacky into the kitchen.

A fresh mug of coffee was waiting for her on the kitchen table. Jacky had found the remains of a packet of ginger nut biscuits and, with incongruous gentility, was arranging them on a plate. The two women sat down facing each other and drank their coffee in silence.

'Don't worry, Catherine.' Unconsciously, Jacky was

reversing their usual roles. 'I'm sure they'll turn up eventually.'

Catherine, absorbed in her own thoughts, ignored the remark. She broke a biscuit in two and dunked it slowly up and down in her coffee. 'Jacky.' She looked up suddenly, as if an idea had just occurred to her. 'Why were you so dogmatic when you were talking to Inspector Mitchell?'

'I suppose it was just seeing you and Brian together so much, I thought — '

'Not about Brian and me,' Gildea interrupted her impatiently. 'That's not important. I meant about the Dodd Effect. You told him it was wrong. What made you say that?'

Jacky looked at her as if she was deranged but, relieved to have her indiscretions dismissed so off-handedly, said eagerly, 'You insisted in one of your lectures that some of his theories were wrong.'

'That's not what I said. I thought some of his ideas were a bit improbable, but that's not the same as being wrong.' Gildea seemed to lose interest in the subject. Her biscuit had collapsed under the strain of prolonged immersion and she was concentrating on fishing bits of it out of her coffee with a teaspoon. 'I suppose Gerry didn't say anything to you about it?'

'About what?' Jacky had lost the thread of the conversation.

'About the Dodd Effect. He didn't tell you it was wrong?'

'Gerry didn't even know about it.' Jacky said with disdain. 'I had to explain it to him.'

'Why?'

'Because in other distinguished academic institutions, such as Cork, the subject is not considered quite as essential or rivetingly interesting as it is here.'

'Jacky!' Gildea banged the teaspoon on the table in

exasperation. 'I didn't mean why didn't he know, I meant why did you have to explain it to him.'

'Because he asked me about it.'

'When?'

'On the nineteenth of January, if you want to know the precise date.' Jacky was looking nervously at her supervisor. 'Are you feeling all right, Catherine? Will I make some more coffee?'

'You're sure about the date?'

'Yes, quite sure. It was Gerry's birthday and I took him out to dinner. We had a long chat about our research projects. I remember because it was really the last time that Gerry would talk to me about his work.'

'Thanks, Jacky. I have to go now.' Gildea stood up abruptly and almost ran out the kitchen. She paused at the door and called back, 'Sorry for leaving you with all the mess. If you do come across Gerry's notes, let me know. Immediately.'

* * *

Mitchell was waiting on the footpath as Catherine Gildea parked the car outside her house. As he moved towards the car, his long shadow fell across the windscreen. She gasped with alarm when he opened the passenger door.

He stuck his head into the car. 'I just want to tell you that I am acting on your suggestion that somebody may have stolen those notebooks from Barry's room.' Even under the sodium vapour lights, he could see she was pale with apprehension.

'Oh Mitch, you frightened me! I thought you were —'

'I'm instituting a search of the O'Meara Building first thing tomorrow,' he interrupted her. He wasn't in any mood for a chat.

'But if somebody stole the notebooks, he wouldn't keep them in the building,' she protested as she climbed un-

197

steadily out of the car. 'He'd get rid of them, surely?'

'You'd be surprised, Dr Gildea, at the incriminating evidence that people keep.'

He walked with her to her gate. 'Tomorrow, when the funeral is over, come back to the department and we'll show you anything we've found,' he told her as she rooted in her pocket for her keys. 'Incidentally, there will be no point in you, or any of your colleagues, coming in before that. I've already stationed a couple of men on the building, and I've given instructions that nobody is to be admitted until we have completed the search.'

'If you're doing all this for my benefit, inspector, I'll try to be suitably grateful.' She had found her keys and was jangling them impatiently in her hand. 'However, I'm quite convinced that the person who killed Brian took those notebooks with him on the night of the murder. I'm prepared to bet you won't find anything interesting in the labs tomorrow!'

17

The common room looked colder by daylight. The curtains were drawn back, revealing a landscape of bycycle racks, dustbins and a concrete shed. Mitchell stood at the window staring fixedly at the brown streaks down the wall where rust from the shed's corrugated iron roof had seeped into the concrete. The cloying drizzle that had persisted all morning was turning to a heavy drenching rain. He picked up *The Irish Times* from the table and turned to the crossword, but then remembered it was Thursday. He knew he wouldn't have the concentration to unravel the cryptic clues. He paced to the door, then back to the window, tossing the folded newspaper into a wastepaper basket as he passed.

Waiting. He seemed to have spent the whole of his life waiting. Waiting for the end of the night shift, waiting for exam results, waiting for news from home during his father's illness. None of them had been as bad as this.

The door opened, but it was only Sam Smith. If you didn't know Sam you'd think from the look of him that he was an insensitive clod. But Sam closed the door silently and stood with his back to it, alert to the tension in the room.

'We'll sit over here, Sam.' Mitchell indicated the table in front of the window. He chose a seat for himself at right angles to the sergeant, so that he had his back to the window and was facing the door.

Sam took his notebook from his pocket, opened a clean page, and set it in front of him on the table. From another pocket he produced a pencil-parer and a pencil and started to sharpen the lead. In the empty building, the small sound made Mitchell's teeth ache. Sam was over-zealous with the parer, and Mitchell heard the point snap. He took his pen from his jacket pocket and handed it to Sam.

'Dr Gildea is here, sir.' A uniformed garda stuck his head round the door.

'Send her in.'

Mitchell had guessed she'd be wearing black, but he hadn't expected the cloak. Drops of moisture clung to the calf-length folds of black wool, giving her a misty outline, like a vision in a Yeats play.

'Sit down, please.' He indicated a chair facing him across the table. His throat was so dry that the remark was probably inaudible, but she must have understood his hand signals, because she walked without hesitation towards him.

Using both hands, she unhooked the bronze clasp at her throat and slipped the cloak from her shoulders. Smith got up hurriedly and took it from her. Round one to Gildea, Mitchell admitted as he watched the sergeant shaking out the folds and draping the cloak carefully over a chair.

Gildea pulled the chair well back from the table before she sat down, and she arranged her skirt fastidiously as she crossed her legs. Her boots were muddy and damp blades of grass stuck to the high heels. 'Well, inspector, do I win my bet? No notebooks?'

For an instant she looked straight into Mitchell's eyes. He lowered his gaze to the polished surface of the table between them. There were no notebooks — only a couple of sheets of notepaper.

'No notebooks.' Now that it was actually happening, he felt detached. Even his anger was gone, leaving only a cold, sarcastic resentment. 'However, if I remember correctly, our little bet was that I would find nothing interesting.' He handed her the two sheets of paper. 'Take a look at this letter. You might find it "interesting".'

She scanned the first page, then glanced at the signature on the second page before starting to read the letter, line by line.

Mitchell had looked forward to seeing her read it, to witnessing the academic façade disintegrate. Now he found he couldn't watch. He took a copy of the letter from his briefcase and read it carefully again:

Dear Catherine,

Further to our conversation last night, I feel I should clarify my position in writing, in case there could be any possible room for confusion about my attitude.

With regard to the experimental work you propose publishing in *The Journal of Molecular Genetics*, I must inform you that I am quite convinced that these results are spurious. At my request, Dr Flynn has recently repeated your most salient experiments, with great care and attention to detail, and not only are his results quite different from those in your manuscript but he can also produce irrefutable evidence that the experiments you claim to have performed could not have been carried out in the way you describe with the equipment currently available to you in this department.

> I am astounded that you have the temerity to
> propose publishing this fraudulent nonsense jointly
> under both our names. Even if you have no regard
> for your own integrity, I would have hoped that, in
> view of our long association, you might show some
> consideration for my scientific reputation and the
> position I hold in this university. However, let me
> hasten to point out that I not only refuse to allow my
> name to be associated with this paper, I must also
> inform you that should you persist in attempting to
> publish the manuscript as drafted, I will have no
> alternative but to inform the journal editors of my
> conviction that your data are false.

As he reached the end of the first page, he looked up at
her. Her face was expressionless but, as she turned to the
second page, her hands were shaking, and both sheets
slipped from her fingers and fluttered slowly to the floor.
Her reflexes didn't seem to be working; she made no
effort to retrieve the pages. She sat staring at her empty
hands until Sam picked up the sheets and gave them
back to her.

Mitchell looked at the second page. He had read the
letter three times already and felt he could recite it by
heart:

> Please believe that it is not my wish to make
> public the dishonesty of your work. I feel that such
> exposure would not be in the best interests of the
> college and I am extremely reluctant to do anything
> that, by bringing the department into disrepute,
> might perhaps reflect badly on other members of
> the staff and influence the future professional
> standing of our graduates. However, I feel I must
> emphasise that, should you refuse to admit the

falsity of your results, I will have no option but to publicly expose you. In the interests of scientific integrity, I believe I have no alternative, however unpleasant the results of this action may be to all concerned. I hope you will give the consequences due consideration before you determine your course of action.

Gildea's face was as white as her silk shirt as she reached the end of the letter and stared at the signature, 'Brian Barry'.

Mitchell held up his hand to forestall any comment. 'Dr Gildea, before you say anything, let me caution you that I regard that letter as highly incriminating and as evidence of a possible motive for Professor Barry's murder. You are not obliged to say anything unless you wish to do so, but anything you do say will be taken down in writing and may be used in evidence.'

His curt tone aroused her from the torpor into which she seemed to have sunk since finishing the letter. 'I will only say, inspector, that I have never seen this letter before today and I have no idea what experimental data are referred to in it.' She was still very pale but her voice was steady.

'You admitted that Professor Barry was reluctant to agree to the publication of some work you had done.' Mitchell hadn't intended to argue with her. The letter spoke for itself: there was no need for further discussion, but he couldn't resist trying to undermine her composure. 'Perhaps it has slipped your mind that you told me that.'

'No, of course I remember.' She was becoming quite flushed, and her eyes sparkled as her passivity yielded to anger.

Mitchell registered, with startling objectivity, how beautiful she was despite her wet hair, her livid cheeks, and the signs of stress around her mouth.

'That was something totally different. Brian never questioned the validity of my results. He was simply too preoccupied to find time to read the manuscript. There was never any question of falsification.' She was breathless with anger, but before Mitchell could reply she gasped, 'Am I allowed to ask where you found this letter?'

'That's a photocopy. The original has been sent for forensic examination. We found it where you left it: in a drawer in your desk. It's ironic that it should have been there, in view of our conversation last night about the improbability of anybody keeping incriminating evidence in the building.' Mitchell was losing his equanimity, and his tone was becoming bitter.

To his surprise, Gildea looked relieved, almost elated, by this reply. I've been to bed with this woman, he thought, and I know nothing about her. I know about her cats, her work, even her sex life, but I don't understand anything that goes on in her mind.

'You found it in my desk? That's all right then. Some-body must have planted it there. Just for one horrible, nightmarish moment when you showed me that letter, I thought you might have found it in Brian's room and that it could possibly have been genuine.' She examined the letter critically. 'You know, inspector, it's a remarkably convincing fake. The signature looks genuine and it couldn't be easy to forge that eccentric scrawl. The style is spot-on too: "scientific integrity" was a great phrase of Brian's. Whoever composed this knew Brian very well; I suppose that exonerates you or your colleagues.'

'Well, Dr Gildea, I don't think we should have any difficulty in establishing the authenticity of the letter. However, that may take a day or two.' He stood up to indicate an end to the interview. 'In the meantime I must ask you not to leave Dublin without advising me and I think you should talk to your solicitor.'

* * *

It took the forensic laboratories just twenty-four hours to authenticate Brian Barry's signature on the letter. Mitchell carried their report in a file under his arm as he pushed his way through the crowd of thirsty barristers surrounding the bar in The Legal Eagle. He found O'Loughlin lunching on a sandwich and a bowl of soup in a quiet corner of the lounge.

'Is it Gildea?' the superintendent asked without preamble.

'It is, sir. The evidence against her seems conclusive.' He sat down beside O'Loughlin and handed him the file. 'The report authenticates Brian Barry's signature and identifies his fingerprints and Gildea's on the letter.' Mitchell looked round distractedly for a waiter but failed to spot one. He lacked the energy to get up in search of a drink. 'You were right. Barry's death was connected with his work.'

O'Loughlin studied the letter carefully, pursing his lips. 'Is this a very serious accusation?'

'Gildea was shocked when I confronted her with it.' He looked at the file resentfully. 'I collected this from the forensic labs myself, so I took the opportunity of consulting the scientists there. They said that this sort of revelation could ruin her career. It would almost certainly constitute valid grounds for dismissal from her lecturership. Even if the university took a lenient view, her reputation as a scientist would be irreparably damaged and she could never publish again, which seems to be the ultimate disgrace. According to them, fear of such a disclosure would certainly constitute an adequate motive for murder.' He glanced up at O'Loughlin and essayed a weak grin. 'They even tried to persuade me that some-body who would fake scientific experiments wouldn't be above murder.'

'All right, Mitch. I'm sorry it has turned out this way.' O'Loughlin sounded genuinely distressed. 'You have been admirably objective under the circumstances.' He knocked out his pipe and stowed it, with his tobacco, in his jacket pocket. 'However, I think I'd better be with you when you confront the lady with that forensic report, and we'll bring along a warrant in case she chooses to be difficult.'

'Funny thing, her keeping damning evidence like that,' he remarked as they left the pub.

'It's horribly ironic.' Mitchell grimaced. 'Only for the fuss she made about those old notebooks, we'd probably never have searched the building again.'

18

There was no reply when the two policemen rang Catherine Gildea's doorbell some hours later.

'I wonder has she given us the slip.' Mitchell peered anxiously through the letterbox. 'There's a back gate from the lane behind the house. If you stay here, sir, I'll take a look around the back and see if there's any light in the house.'

The cold damp air was threatening to reactivate O'Loughlin's rheumatism as he shifted his weight from one foot to another and waited for Mitchell to return. After five minutes he heard footsteps in the hall and the door was opened by Mitchell, who looked dishevelled and dismayed.

'Be careful, sir. The house is full of gas. I looked through the kitchen window and saw Gildea lying with her head in the oven. I broke the window and climbed in,' he explained breathlessly as he led the way down the stairs to the kitchen. 'She's still alive, so I've called an ambulance.

'Do you know, sir, I warned her that it was dangerous not to have bars on that window. Now it's probably saved her life.' He had brought a blanket from the bedroom and was wrapping it around Catherine Gildea's inert body.

'I wonder if she'll thank you when she comes round?'

* * *

As they watched the ambulance crew carry the stretcher down the steps, O'Loughlin laid a restraining hand on Mitchell's shoulder. 'I'll go with the ambulance and phone for a bangharda to meet me at the hospital. You stay here and tidy up. Then go home and get some rest. You must have got a bellyful of gas while you were rescuing her. You look terrible.'

'It's just shock, sir. All the time I was trying to convince you that she was guilty, part of me must have been hoping she wasn't,' he admitted with uncharacteristic frankness. 'I'll stay here for a while and fix the window.' He turned back through the front door, his shoulders sagging. 'Maybe you'd be kind enough to phone me and let me know how she is,' he called after O'Loughlin, but he wasn't sure whether the superintendent had heard him.

For a while, Mitchell busied himself finding pieces of timber, a hammer and nails. He hurriedly boarded over the broken window before he realised there was no urgency in the situation. After the emotional pressure of the last few days, he felt tired and listless. He could go home and phone the hospital from there but could not summon up the energy to leave the house.

Watson and Crick, sensing that something was wrong, were screaming madly around his feet. He found an open tin of pet food in the fridge and fed them, which seemed to be all they wanted. He thought of making himself a cup of coffee but there wasn't any instant coffee and the percolator was too much bother.

He wandered aimlessly upstairs and sat in an armchair in the front room. The house felt cold and empty, and the worn furniture seemed hostile. The only welcoming object, on a silver tray with two glasses beside it, was a bottle of Crested Ten. The seal was unbroken; she must have bought it recently. He remembered telling her it was his favourite whiskey.

'Well, girl, you won't miss it, wherever you're going,' he said aloud. Tearing open the seal, he poured a generous measure into one of the glasses. As he put it to his lips, the doorbell rang. He gulped down the neat whiskey and guiltily replaced the glass on the tray.

'Am I interrupting something, inspector?' Jacky Whelan was smiling roguishly at him on the doorstep. 'Catherine asked me to let her know immediately if I found a copy of Gerry's notes. Can I come in for a minute?'

'Jacky, I'm sorry.' He felt awkward and wasn't sure what to tell her. 'There's been an accident. They've taken Catherine to the hospital.'

'Is she all right? Is it serious?'

'I don't know, Jacky,' he replied tonelessly.

'Can I go and see her?' She brandished a file of papers frantically at him. 'These notes are really urgent.'

'No, you can't possibly see her,' he snapped. 'What have you got there anyway?'

'It's a photocopy of Gerry's notebook. You know,' detecting his lack of enthusiasm, 'the one that was stolen from Brian's office on the night of the murder.'

'Look, you'd better come in. The neighbours have had enough excitement for one day.' He led her into the sitting room and plugged in a small electric fire.

'I stole some of Catherine's whiskey. I suppose you could have some too.' He poured tots into both glasses and handed one to Jacky.

'Are you sure she won't mind, inspector?' She seemed alarmed by the audacity of the gesture.

'Jacky, I don't think Catherine will be coming back

209

here.' He tried to adopt a fatherly tone but the attempt was unsuccessful and his voice sounded funereal.

'Is she dead, inspector?' The possibility dawned on Jacky for the first time.

'Sit down, love. I might as well tell you the whole story. Everybody will know tomorrow.' Seeing the apprehension on Jacky's face, he asked in a gentler voice, 'You were close to Catherine, weren't you?'

'I liked her a lot. She was always nagging me but she was the only member of staff who took me seriously.' Jacky sat down on the edge of one of the armchairs. 'Even Brian thought I was just a joke. I know I act the clown a lot, but that's only to cover up my inadequacies. Catherine says she thinks I'll never be a real scientist but at least she helped me to try.' Embarrassed by her own admissions, she took a gulp of whiskey, catching her breath as the strong spirit hit her gullet.

'Inspector, you look so depressed.' There were tears in Jacky's eyes. Mitchell couldn't tell whether they were caused by the whiskey or by emotion. 'Is she dead?'

'She tried to kill herself.' He had brought his voice under control. 'We found her in the kitchen with all the gas taps turned on. She'd have blown the house sky high by Monday if the super and I hadn't arrived in time to save her.'

'Wasn't she lucky you got here at just the right moment?' Her worst fears allayed, Jacky wiped her eyes with the back of her hand and was ready to enjoy the drama of the situation.

'Maybe it would have been better if we had arrived ten minutes later.' He knew he really should not tell her, but he needed to talk about it to somebody . 'She killed Barry.'

'No, inspector! That's not possible. They were terribly close.' Jacky was outraged. 'Honestly, I know she adored him. She never said so, but I know from the way she

210

talked about him. A woman can always tell,' she added confidingly. 'Why would she kill him?'

Receiving no reply from the accuser, she continued desperately, 'You've no proof! Just because she found the body, you think she murdered him. Frankly, I don't believe a word of it. It's all nonsense!' As a gesture of defiance, she flounced over to the sideboard and poured herself another large whiskey. Still eliciting no reply from the inspector, she sat down again, glass in hand, and glared at him.

'We know that she faked some experimental data,' Mitchell responded eventually. He was hoarse and he realised he wasn't far from tears. He wished Jacky would go away and stop tormenting him. 'Barry found out and he threatened to tell everybody.'

'That's rubbish!' Jacky wasn't prepared to entertain the notion. 'In the first place, Katy is dead straight. She tore strips off Peter for suggesting that he might include some dubious results in his report. Secondly, Brian would never have done anything to damage Katy. He was crazy about her.'

Mitchell got up abruptly and fetched his briefcase from the hall. He extracted the letter and handed it to her. 'You might as well look at this.'

Her assurance evaporated a little as she scanned the text. 'That's awful,' she whispered. However, she recovered quickly and returned to the attack. 'That's just a copy. I bet it's a fake. Where did you get it?'

'We have the original,' he said patiently, 'and we've checked that the signature is genuine. I found it in Catherine's desk when we searched her office yesterday morning.'

'Which drawer was it in?' Jacky was relentless.

'Damn it, Jacky, what does it matter where it was?' His voice was breaking and he tried to sound angry instead. 'For what it's worth, it was in the middle drawer.'

'You planted it!'

'Don't be ridiculous.' He was growing weary of this endless interrogation. 'You read too many detective stories. We don't plant evidence and, frankly, if I was planting evidence I wouldn't have chosen Catherine's desk. At one stage I was a bit crazy about her too.'

This admission failed to arouse Jacky's usual fascination with romance and she eyed him coldly. 'If you didn't plant the letter, somebody else did. It wasn't in Catherine's desk on Wednesday night.'

'How do you — ' he started to ask. 'Of course, the nightly exploration of the desk.' For a moment, he was interested, but relapsed rapidly into gloom again. 'Good try, Jacky, but the desk was locked yesterday, so you couldn't have inspected the contents on Wednesday night.'

Jacky dismissed this objection. 'Catherine always locks the top drawer, that's where she keeps confidential files, but she never bothers locking the others. The middle drawer was open on Wednesday evening and Owen O'Neill and I had a glance through it. Anybody could have put the letter there later that night, after we'd gone, and then just slammed the drawer. Once the top drawer is locked, the others lock automatically when they're pushed home. You don't have to be a detective to work that out,' she finished patronisingly.

'Are you sure this letter wasn't there on Wednesday?'

'Absolutely positive. Ask Owen if you don't believe me. All the staff had gone to Mrs Barry's house from the church, so we were safe from any interruption. We were looking for the minutes of Monday's staff meeting to see what was decided about our future. We had to go through everything before we were sure they weren't there.'

'Maybe you saw the letter but decided it was personal

212

and didn't examine it?' Mitchell suggested as a last resort.

Jacky looked at him scathingly and didn't bother to reply.

Mitchell was tempted to ignore Jacky's information. He was tired, the case was closed, the loose ends tied up. But he felt a stirring of excitement as the significance of this new evidence became clear.

'That letter has to be a fake.' Jacky cut across his thoughts. 'Let me see it again.'

He handed it to her. While she studied it he took the forensic report from his briefcase. 'Catherine's prints are quite clear on the front page and there's a nice set of Barry's just under his signature,' he summarised the report for Jacky, but really he was arguing with himself.

'It doesn't make sense.' Jacky threw the pages on the ground and went to stand at the window, staring vacantly into the dusk.

A page had fallen at Mitchell's feet. He picked it up and mindlessly read it yet again. 'Look at this page again, Jacky. It makes no specific reference to Catherine, or to her work. It could have been written to any colleague.' He tried not to betray his growing hope.

Jacky perched on the arm of his chair and read over his shoulder. 'You're suggesting that the back page is genuine but the front page is a fake.' She picked up the other page and scrutinised it eagerly.

But Mitchell had already lost faith in his idea. 'It's a nice theory but the forensic lab would have noticed if the typeface was different on the two pages.'

'No, they're obviously the same,' Jacky said confidently. 'I recognise the typeface. That's the departmental printer. Anybody could retype the front page and print it on that.'

'How do we explain Catherine's fingerprints on the front page?'

Jacky contemplated the problem for a couple of minutes before suggesting, 'She always keeps a stack of notepaper on her desk. Anybody could have taken a sheet. The top sheet might have her prints on it — whoever took it couldn't be sure, but there would be a fair chance.'

'If the back page is genuine, Jacky —'

'Somebody else on the staff had a motive for killing Barry,' she completed the sentence, her eyes shining at the dramatic potential of the situation.

'Which one?'

She looked blank.

'What about those famous notes you were clutching when you arrived? Why was Catherine so anxious to find them?'

'I've only glanced at them. They look very dull, but Catherine was desperate to see them. They must have some connection with Brian's death.' She jumped up and retrieved the file from the sideboard where she had abandoned it.

'I was lucky to find them,' she said as she started to examine the contents. 'I met the landlord as I was coming in from college. Gerry and himself are great pals — they're both fanatical bird-watchers. He asked how Gerry was getting on in Switzerland and said not to let Gerry forget about the papers he had left in his safe. I had to swear it was a matter of life and death before he would give them to me. I didn't realise how true that would turn out to be!'

'See if you can discover what they're all about, while I ring the hospital.'

Mitchell returned from the phone looking jubilant. 'She's going to pull through. We found her just in time. She hasn't come round yet, but the doctors say she's as strong as an ox and will have recovered by tomorrow. Now, anything coming from those notes?'

'Mitch, give me a break! While you're waiting, could you make me a cup of coffee. I think I may have had too much of that whiskey. My head is starting to spin.'

'Maybe there's still some gas around,' he suggested charitably.

* * *

An hour and three cups of coffee later, Mitchell was lying on Catherine's bed, waiting for Jacky to finish deciphering the notes. With the fidelity characteristic of their species, Watson and Crick had accepted him as a surrogate for Catherine and were purring happily into both his ears. Eventually he lost patience and returned to the front room, where Jacky was sitting on the rug in front of the electric fire. Sheets of paper were spread all around her and she was frowning with concentration. 'I don't know if these can tell us anything.'

'You must have some idea after reading all this.' He stepped with exaggerated care between the pages.

'They're only graphs and tables with a few experimental details and the occasional comment,' Jacky moaned. 'It will take hours before I'm sure what it all means.'

'You have some idea?'

'It's only an idea,' Jacky was cautious, 'but it seems very unlikely.'

'Jacky, the circumstances are pretty improbable.' Mitchell sat down on the floor beside her and tried to look over her shoulder. 'Tell me what you think.'

'All right, but don't blame me if it sounds ridiculous.' The cats were now both sitting on the papers at Jacky's feet. She absently dislodged them to find the sheets she needed. 'I told Catherine on Monday that I thought Gerry was repeating experiments already carried out by Peter McCormack. He seems to have started doing that just after Christmas.' She tapped her teeth nervously with a pencil. 'Catherine must have guessed the truth, because

215

she asked me if Gerry had said anything about Conor Dodd's work. I see now what was in her mind. If I'm interpreting Gerry's results correctly, it looks as if he has disproved all Conor's recent findings.' She looked up hopefully at Mitchell, but he didn't know what to say. 'That would be pretty sensational,' she insisted. 'Peter, of course, was too naïve to understand the implications of his own results and Brian couldn't let him put something so potentially explosive in an undergraduate thesis. When Gerry got the same results, Brian must have been sure that Dodd's recent papers were faked.'

Jacky was beginning to get excited now and to have more faith in her own theories. 'Knowing Brian, he would have immediately challenged Noddy with these results, hence the letter.' She looked up at Mitchell to make sure he was following her reasoning. He wasn't, but he nodded encouragingly. 'Dodd was in danger of exposure, so he shot Brian and removed the incriminating evidence — Gerry's and Peter's notebooks — from Brian's office. He probably thought that he was safe, until Catherine made a fuss about the missing notebooks.'

'He must have realised that she was beginning to suspect the truth.' Things were falling rapidly into place in Mitchell's mind. 'Of course! He was there on Wednesday evening when I caught Catherine going through Barry's desk. Obviously, Dodd believed she was looking for the notebooks even though I didn't!' He threw himself into an armchair. A cat immediately jumped on his knee. 'So he decided to try to incriminate her.'

He stroked the cat thoughtfully. 'Jacky, what time was it when you finished rifling through Catherine's desk on Wednesday night?'

'We went straight back to the lab from the church. That would have been about seven o'clock. I chatted to Owen for a while before we decided to take a look in

Catherine's desk. That couldn't have taken more than half an hour. We went for a drink afterwards, and it was just before eight o'clock when we got to the bar.'

'Catherine and I left Barry's soon after eight o'clock,' Mitchell recalled. 'If Conor Dodd left right after us, he would have had about two hours to fake that letter, put it in Catherine's desk and be clear of the department before the uniformed lads arrived to close the building.'

Jacky was now the one who was doubtful. 'There are two things I don't understand. First, how did Dodd manage to kill Brian in his office when he was supposed to be lecturing to a packed audience in the Burlington?'

'That's no problem,' Mitchell assured her. 'The murder took place about twenty minutes after the end of his lecture. It would have been easy enough for Dodd to slip out, drive to the college, kill Barry, and be back in the Burlington in time to circulate with the sherry drinkers for a few minutes before dinner.' Mitchell sat back in the armchair and lit a cigarette. 'What's your second problem, my dear Watson?'

'If that letter is a fake and Catherine is innocent, why did she try to kill herself?'

'I don't think she did. We have a murderer on the loose and he probably tried to kill Catherine too.' The extent of his own responsibility for the situation began to dawn on him. 'All he had to do was call to see her, knock her out when her back was turned, and lay her out neatly in the oven with the gas turned on. He would calculate that the letter, followed by her suicide, would be sufficient evidence to convince everybody of her guilt.'

'His calculation wasn't too far off. He very nearly succeeded.' Jacky too was subdued, as if realising for the first time that drama isn't always pleasant.

* * *

217

'Now, young lady, I'm sending you home in garda custody. Sergeant Smith is on his way with a search warrant for Dodd's house. He'll take you home and stay with you until I've seen Dodd. You know far too much for your own good. We have enough dead and dying geneticists on our hands for one week. I don't want another.'

Despite Jacky's protests, he steered her down the steps to the waiting car. 'I promise to let you know as soon as anything happens. I'm grateful for your detective work tonight. If you ever decide that genetics isn't for you, think about joining the Garda. I'll give you a good reference.'

He bundled her unceremoniously into the back of the car. 'Sam, take this woman home and stay with her. She is not to go out or make any phone calls. Get a bangharda to take over from you if it looks like being an overnight stint.'

As Sam waited to pull out into the traffic, Jacky rolled down the window and called to Mitchell, 'Inspector, did you really mean what you said?'

'About the reference?'

'No, about Catherine. Are you really crazy about her?'

'Sam, take this woman out of my sight immediately, and, for your own sake, tell her nothing about your private life.'

Jacky, as always, had the last word, as the car pulled away from the kerb. 'Good night, inspector, and good hunting — for the murderer, I mean.'

* * *

It was just after midnight when the phone rang. Jacky beat the sergeant to it by a length.

'Jacky, you were right!' Mitchell was elated. 'We found Barry's briefcase in the boot of Dodd's car. Everything was in it: the missing notebooks, the other half of the

218

letter and the draft of an article that Barry was writing denouncing Dodd's recent papers.'

'Any word about Catherine?'

'Yes, I rang the hospital just now. She came round about half an hour ago. They sedated her again immediately but they expect she'll be well enough for visitors tomorrow. You can see her — but not until after lunch. I want to talk to her first. Incidentally, I'm afraid you lose your police escort now that we have Dodd under lock and key.'

'Oh, no, I don't. Sam's in the middle of telling me all about you. I'm not letting him go until he finishes that!' She glanced archly at the sergeant before continuing, 'Anyway he's rather dishy, so I just might hold on to him until tomorrow.'

'What about poor Gerry?'

' "Poor Gerry", as you call him, is lying in the sun in the Cyclades and, if I know Gerry, is probably also lying to some bronzed Rhine-maiden. What he doesn't know won't hurt him!'

* * *

'Katy, are you all right?' Mitchell approached the bedside cautiously, but she seemed to be asleep. He stood looking down at her; she looked less ill than he had expected, but her good colour was probably the result of carbon monoxide poisoning rather than robust good health. She opened an eye and examined him silently.

'I'll do all the apologising you want in a minute,' he said penitently, 'but first you must tell me what happened last night.'

'I'm not sure. I've been trying to remember all morning.' Pulling herself up into a sitting position, she looked furtively around. 'Have you got a cigarette, for the love of God?' He lit one for her and she dragged on it hungrily.

219

'The last thing that I'm clear about is that the doorbell rang. I called out, "Who's there" and a man's voice said, "Police." I'd been more or less expecting you to come and arrest me, so I opened the door. There was nobody to be seen, so I went out onto the step. Somebody grabbed me and pushed me back into the house. I remember the smell of ether. The next thing I knew I woke up in this bed. I gather from the nurses that I'm supposed to have gassed myself.'

She looked around helplessly for an ashtray. Mitchell found an empty matchbox in his pocket and offered it to her. 'I had a rather mysterious conversation with the consultant psychiatrist this morning. I thought he was helping me through the trauma of nearly being a murder victim, while he was trying to discover why I tried to kill myself. We both became very confused.' She laughed weakly. 'How did I escape the gas oven?'

'You were right. I came back with a warrant for your arrest.' He explained how he had found her.

'I suppose I should thank you for saving my life,' she said grudgingly and turned her head away from him.

'You should really thank those wretched cats of yours. The fact that the cat door was open probably let enough gas escape to save you — if it hadn't been for that you'd be in the mortuary by now.'

'I'm glad to be still around, Mitch, but I don't suppose you believe me about the ether.'

'Certainly I do. I can even tell you who administered it, but I suppose you know that yourself.'

'Was it Conor?' She turned her head towards him, but she didn't sound very interested.

'Yes, we have him in custody and there's plenty of evidence. You suspected him, didn't you?'

She nodded but still seemed indifferent.

'Catherine, we'll talk about this again when you're

fully recovered.' He took the butt of her cigarette, put it out under the tap and hid it in the matchbox. 'I'd better go now; I promised the doctor I'd only stay for five minutes. He was already muttering "police harassment" when I insisted on seeing you this morning.' He was about to kiss her, when the door opened and a large bunch of roses appeared, followed by Jacky's head.

'Oh damn, inspector, I didn't know you were here. I was going to tell Catherine that these were from you!'

Mitchell touched Catherine's hand. 'I must go. Jacky will tell you everything you want to know about what happened while you were out for the count.'

19

'Mitch, please stop treating me like an invalid,' Catherine protested, the third time he asked if she was sure she wasn't sitting in a draught. 'I'm perfectly fit again.'

Mitchell looked at her critically and was forced to admit that she looked well. Her appearance was so changed, he had almost walked past her when he arrived at the restaurant. Her hair was cut in a new style which brought some of it forward onto her face, leaving the remainder caught behind her head with a narrow ribbon. The candlelight picked up an auburn tint in her hair, which he suspected was also new.

He decided that the black velvet trousers she was wearing actually looked more feminine than the well-cut skirts she normally wore.

She put down her glass. 'You'll be able to do an identi-kit of me.'

He realised he had been staring at her. 'I hope you're not overdoing things. You ought to be taking it easy,' he said quickly, to cover his embarrassment.

'You sound like Bob Roche.' She imitated the professor's orotund tones, '"You should take things easy, Catherine, my dear. You've had a very trying time, physically and emotionally," and could I possibly see my way to taking Conor's lectures as well as Brian's. He'd do them himself, of course, but for a meeting in Brussels. It also happens that Fairyhouse is on next week!'

'Poor old Roche, you have him taped!' Mitchell laughed nervously. He was very uncertain how the evening would turn out. In fact, right this minute he wished he'd never suggested it. Catherine's manner was warm and bright — maybe too bright, almost brittle, but perhaps she was nervous too. He searched his mind for something to say.

'Did you know that Roche and myself are past pupils of the same school?'

'That figures,' she retorted cryptically, as she turned her attention to the menu.

'What would you like to order?'

'Some information, please,' she came back smartly.

'Surely Jacky's told you everything by now?' Mitchell was reluctant to embark on a discussion of the case so early in the evening. He looked around desperately for a waiter.

'Of course she has. By the way, Mitch, did you promise that youngster you would help her get a job as a detective?'

'I said something of the sort,' he said cautiously. 'She's taking me seriously?'

'She's been full of it, all week. Of course she's taken a great shine to your sergeant. That might partly explain her enthusiasm, but she is genuinely interested and it mightn't be such a bad idea.' She sipped her drink pensively. 'Jacky's never going to make it in research. Her mind is sharp enough and,' she raised her eyebrows theatrically, 'as we both know, she is full of natural curiosity, but science is too abstract for her.'

'Well, if she's serious about the idea, tell her to come and talk to me,' he said absently as a waiter finally appeared to take their order.

223

'Why did Conor kill Brian?' Catherine asked bluntly as soon as the waiter had left.

Mitchell produced a folded sheet of paper from his wallet and handed it to her without comment.

Her hands shook as she unfolded the page and held it away from her to catch the light from the single candle on the table.

Dear Conor,

Further to our recent conversation, I feel I must make my position clear to you in case, in the heat of our exchange, there might have been room for misunderstanding.

As you know, I have always admired the pioneering work you did in the sixties on growth rate control. However, as I explained to you, in the course of work in my own laboratory we recently had reason to test some of your published conclusions on the relationship between cAMP and growth rate. Our data, copies of which I showed you, clearly conflict with the conclusions in your recent publications and the evidential data that you quote.

Despite your repeated denials, I am reluctantly forced to the conclusion that your results are spurious. Furthermore, since our conversation I have reread your papers, particularly the methodology of your cAMP measurements, and it occurs to me that, since the type of high-pressure chromatography apparatus that you describe was not available anywhere in the college until I purchased one last October, it would not have been possible for you to carry out the measurements in the way you claim.

I reiterate the verbal offer I made to you, that we should jointly publish a paper, admitting 'error' in the published data and presenting the correct results. However, I must emphasise that my willingness to do this is contingent upon your agreement to decline the offer of the Institute medal. I feel that, under the present circumstances, it would make a mockery of the Institute centenary were you to accept the medal and present a paper on your so-called research.

I had hoped that by this morning's council meeting you might have indicated to the Institute that you could not accept the medal at this juncture. Let me stress that, should you persist in the charade of accepting the medal and presenting a paper at the centenary function, I shall have no choice but to publish the results obtained in this laboratory in a paper refuting all your recent work. Let me add that, if you insist on addressing the centenary meeting I shall absent myself from it and shall instead occupy myself in drafting a refutation of your work.

Catherine had paled visibly beneath her make-up and seemed almost as shaken as when Mitchell had confronted her with the forged letter. 'Poor old Conor,' she said with genuine pity, 'what a choice: either to turn down the coveted medal or be publicly denounced.'

'Was it a serious threat?'

'Oh, yes. Brian would have gone through with it. He hated anything crooked and was quite evangelistic in his determination to uphold high standards among the scientific community.'

'Surely being wrong isn't such a serious sin?' Mitchell objected.

'God, no! We're all guilty of being wrong, in almost every paper we publish. Usually it's just rash conclusions that the data don't support and unlikely predictions based on insufficient evidence. Journal editors are supposed to elimate hyperbole but they allow a little poetic licence. You set the record straight in subsequent papers. You never, of course, admit to having been wrong; you just modify your hypothesis to fit the latest results.'

'But faked data are rare?' Mitchell was intrigued.

'Probably, but of course nobody knows. We're only aware of those authors, like Conor, who are found out, and that occurs infrequently. However, the pressure put on academics by the "publish or perish" philosophy is bound to increase the temptation to invent data. In Conor's case the stimulus was proably the prospect of getting Roche's chair. Conor had published very little in his middle years and he needed a substantial addition to his list if he was to be in serious contention for the professorship, so he simply made some up. Then, being awarded the Institute medal would have made him virtually a certainty for the chair. It was an offer he couldn't refuse.'

Catherine shook her head thoughtfully. 'Had Conor turned down the medal and agreed to Brian's offer of a joint publication, nothing worse than minor embarrassment would have ensued. However, if Brian had carried out his threat to publish a refutation in which he openly accused Conor of faking data, that would have been a major scandal. It might have ruined Conor for life and certainly would have finished his chances of getting the chair.'

Catherine paused while the waiter proffered a bottle of wine for Mitchell's approval, but once he'd withdrawn, couldn't resist pointing out, 'You accepted a similar threat as a credible motive for murder, when you thought I was guilty!'

Mitchell blushed deeply and sat in chastened silence

until Catherine rescued the conversation by asking, 'Has Conor confessed?'

'He denies everything. He's been remanded to a psychiatric hospital; I suspect he may be quite mad.' He absently tasted the wine and nodded to the waiter. 'When did you start suspecting Conor?'

'I was never sure,' she said hesitantly, 'but don't forget that I had one great advantage over you.'

He shook his head questioningly. 'I knew I hadn't done it,' she explained with an uneasy grin.

'Seriously, why Conor?'

She buttered a piece of roll and nibbled it. 'It was the missing notebooks. If you'd known Brian,' she insisted almost passionately, 'you'd know how scrupulously careful, almost neurotic, he was with other people's notes and manuscripts. Once I was sure that they weren't in Brian's office or in his study at home, I was certain somebody had stolen them. I wouldn't have made the connection with Conor if it hadn't been for those journals that Brian had on loan from the library.' She paused deliberately, contemplating the steaming bowl of mussels that a waiter had just placed in front of her.

Mitchell said nothing while he sprinkled salt and pepper on his steak, annoyed to find himself on the receiving end of delaying tactics.

Catherine carefully detached a mussel from its shell and chewed it critically. 'These are excellent. I wonder where they get them.'

Mitchell was not to be so easily distracted. 'Tell me about the journals, Catherine.'

'Oh, yes, the journals.' Catherine was obviously enjoying herself. 'You see, scientific journals are like other periodicals. They go out of date very quickly. Libraries must keep back numbers, but they're rarely consulted. They're used by students writing theses or, as in my case, by lecturers who need to refer to classic papers. So,' realising that her audience was getting restive, she came to the point, 'when I was returning all those old volumes from Brian's office to the library, I couldn't help wondering why he had them. I looked at the indexes and saw that every volume contained an article by Conor. Collectively, those volumes contained the papers in which Conor described the Dodd Effect.'

'Why didn't you tell me?' Mitchell made no effort to disguise his reproach. 'You'd have saved us both a lot of trouble.'

'Would you have believed me?' She put down her fork and looked him in the eye. When he refused to reply, she admitted, 'I didn't really believe it myself. My theory seemed improbable and my evidence nebulous. If Gerry had been here it would have been easy to prove, but presumably Brian deliberately sent him off until the situation with Conor had been resolved.'

Mitchell nodded. 'I've spoken to Gerry; he's back in Zürich. He confirms that the trouble started with the experiments that Peter McCormack designed for himself, in Barry's absence. They were really testing Dodd's theories. Peter got the wrong answer: quite the opposite to results that Dodd himself had recently published. Barry saw their significance when he read Peter's report during the Christmas holiday. He scared Peter off pursuing the project, but asked Gerry to repeat the experiments. He didn't tell him why, but Gerry soon began to see their significance in relation to Dodd's work. He mentioned this to Barry, got his head bitten off, and the next thing he knew he was on a plane to Zürich.'

'And Brian presented Conor with Gerry's results.' Catherine took up the narrative. 'No wonder Brian had been preoccupied since Christmas.'

'The letter to Dodd is dated the sixteenth of February,'

Mitchell confirmed, 'so the confrontation must have taken place about three weeks before the murder. Dodd must have stolen the gun some time before the twenty-fourth, when Roche first noticed that it was missing, probably on the twenty-first, during Roche's birthday party.'

'Oh, yes, I was there myself,' she confirmed eagerly, 'but of course you know that.' Her enthusiasm faded. 'Why didn't he shoot Brian as soon as he had the gun?'

'He may not have had many opportunities. You said yourself that the building was nearly always full of people. From Dodd's point of view the night of his lecture was ideal. He expected all the staff to be at his lecture and, as it happened, the postgraduates would be at the wedding party. In addition, the lecture gave him an alibi.'

'How did he know that Brian would be in his office?'

'We're not sure, but Peter McCormack admits he was bellyaching at coffee about having to work late because Barry was going to be there. Dodd's students were scandalised that Barry wouldn't be attending the centenary lecture, and Dodd may well have overheard them talking about it. Alternatively, he may have interpreted Barry's threat to use the time to draft a refutation as meaning literally that he would be working on it in his office — correctly, as it turned out.'

'So that was what he was doing when I interrupted him.'

'Catherine.' Mitchell pushed his chair back so that he was looking up at her. 'Why did you lie to me about that?'

'I didn't lie,' she protested, too quickly.

'You had a row with Barry hadn't you?'

'He'd had a manuscript of mine for ages,' she said defensively. 'There were several references to Dodd's recent publications in it, and of course Brian couldn't let

229

me publish it like that, but he didn't explain that to me. I thought he hadn't bothered to read it.'

Mitchell said nothing but lit two cigarettes and handed her one.

'I was very bitchy to him,' she admitted shamefacedly. She drew nervously on her cigarette and tried to tap non-existent ash into the empty mussel shells on her plate. 'That's why I didn't tell you. I couldn't face the realisation that, after so many years working together, my last words to Brian had been so nasty.' She stubbed out the cigarette in disgust. 'How did you know?'

'Peter McCormack heard you.'

The waiter removed their plates, without comment, as if aware of the tension between them. Catherine waved away the menu. 'Just coffee, please.' Mitchell nodded aquiesence and they both stared silently at the tablecloth until coffee was served.

'How do I say I'm sorry?' Mitchell said with unusual humility, as he spooned sugar into his cup.

'Mitch, you don't have to —' She started to speak but he stopped her.

'Please, let me tell you how I feel. That one night we had together was great.' She was silent, listening to him, leaving her coffee untouched. 'I never thought things could be that simple between a man and a woman.' He picked up his dessert spoon and turned it over and back between his hands, examining it as if he hadn't come across one before. 'Catherine, meeting you was the best bloody thing that ever happened to me,' he said despairingly, 'and I had to go and screw it up!'

She didn't say anything. Her eyes were fixed on the tablecloth and her fingers played with the stem of her glass.

'I'm asking you, in my inarticulate way, could we start again, in spite of everything that's happened?'

230

She remained silent, a look of pain on her face.

'Catherine, I know I'm only an ignorant, flat-footed copper. I suppose I'm no match for a woman of your education.'

She banged the glass down on the table and burst out angrily, 'Mitch, for Christ's sake stop it! Stop running yourself down!'

He looked at her in amazement, but before he could reply she said firmly, 'No, Mitch. I thought at one stage that we could be good for each other. Even the night Brian died, I found myself attracted to you.' She was being consciously blunt. 'I don't regret the night we spent together, but we couldn't start again.'

'I know how you feel.' He was watching her closely, trying to fathom her reactions. 'I suppose it was hoping too much, to ask you to forget that I accused you of murder.'

'No, I could probably get over that,' she said confidently. 'You were only doing your job. Accepting your invitation to dinner was a way of telling you that.'

Mitchell shook his head, unable to follow her argument.

'Anyway,' she insisted, 'the psychologists say that murder is the one crime of which we are all capable. I think I find it harder to accept that you accused me of faking scientific results!' She drank some coffee, watching him across the rim of her cup.

'The situation wasn't easy for me,' he pleaded. 'I was still in love with you even when I was convinced you must have killed Barry.'

'But don't you see, that's just the point.' She put down her cup. 'You didn't suspect me despite loving me; you suspected me because you loved me!'

He looked at her blankly, and she tried to explain, 'There was never any benefit of the doubt for me; you would have regarded that as self-indulgence. You had

231

persuaded yourself I was guilty long before you found that letter.'

'O'Loughlin accused me of that too.' Mitchell, out of his depth, sounded innocently surprised.

'I don't really blame you for it, Mitch.' She was trying to minimise the pain she was inflicting. 'You were only trying to do your duty as you saw it, but I couldn't live on those terms.'

She looked up at him in an effort to make him understand, but he could find nothing to say. She dropped her eyes and picked up her glass again, turning it to catch the reflection of the candlelight. 'I've spent the last twelve years in the shadow of a perfectionist,' she said very softly, 'and all I've got to show for it now is a lot of pain. I'm tired of being shackled to such a weight of duty. I want to live on the bright side of the street for a while.'

He didn't know what to answer. He offered her another cigarette, but she shook her head absently. 'Mitch,' she said suddenly, 'you do a difficult, dirty job and you do it well. You do it with little recognition and with less reward. Stop being a begrudger and learn to like yourself.'

'I came here tonight with a dozen excuses for what happened, but I've no answer to these charges.' He pushed back his chair and stood up. 'Come on, I'd better take you home.'